The CAFE Club

Here Comes The Sun!

Ann Bryant

Hippo

Scholastic Children's Books,
Commonwealth House, 1–19 New Oxford Street,
London WC1A 1NU, UK
a division of Scholastic Ltd
London ~ New York ~ Toronto ~ Sydney ~ Auckland

First published in the UK by Scholastic Ltd, 1998

ISBN 0 590 19902 1

Typeset by Rowland Phototypesetting Ltd,
Bury St Edmunds, Suffolk
Printed by Cox & Wyman Ltd, Reading, Berks.

Chapter 1

Andy

Hi! It's Andy speaking – the one they call the daring one. Right now, though, my courage is being put to the test. So far I've held out without being sick and without having to lie down. In this self-service cafe there's only me and one man who are still reasonably upright. I doubt I could make it to the loo even if I wanted to, because Leah is lying on my right foot and I don't want to disturb her if I can help it. The problem is that my right foot has now gone to sleep. In fact, I would say it's in a deep coma.

Let me explain. The six of us girls in the Cafe Club are on a boat on our way to France. Unfortunately we've chosen a terrible day to begin our great adventure, because we are crossing the English Channel in a force-ten gale. I've done this crossing lots of times before, but I've never known a crossing as rough as this. The cafe where I'm sitting had to close about half an hour ago because all the crockery and glasses and everything kept crashing to the floor and smashing as the boat tipped violently from side to side. Someone once told me that if you put your feet on a bag, or anything other than the floor, you're less likely to get seasick. I've got one foot on my rucksack, but, as I said, the other foot is firmly wedged under Leah.

Since the others are in no fit state to tell you about themselves, or each other – or about anything, actually – *I* will. I'll start with my very best friend, Leah Bryan (currently half-dead under the table). Leah is the musician. She is extremely talented and is sure to be a professional musician at some stage. She has no confidence in herself at all, though, and worries about everything. As far as looks are concerned, she's the complete opposite to me. I've got very short dark hair and Leah's got very long blonde hair. I've got dark skin, Leah's got fair skin. I've got brown eyes, Leah's got bluey-grey eyes. I'm very small, Leah's medium height. Even our families are very different. I've got one baby brother, Sebastien, Leah's got one fifteen-year-old sister, Kim.

There's one other thing I haven't told you about myself, and that is that I'm half French. Mum is French and Dad is English, but works in France. I should also confess right here that though I'm supposed to be so daring, with the reputation that nothing scares me, there *is* one thing that does. Not a thing, actually – a person. My dad. We've had our moments of being close to each other, but most of the time we're not close. Dad is very highly principled and far too strict. He's out of touch, to tell the truth. Out of touch with youth and out of touch with me, because he's not at home enough. Mum adores him and would never cross him. In a way she's out of touch too, because of her blinding love for Dad. All the same, strange as it may seem, I love them both.

Just outside this cafeteria, her foot sticking out at the

perfect angle to trip up unsuspecting, lurching passengers, is Luce, short for Lucy Edmunson, the crazy one. She's even crazy in her sleep. I can't think of another single person I know who would have managed to crash out in such an inconvenient place. Luce has frizzy – no, sorry, we're not allowed to say that – curly, auburny-blonde hair, bluey-grey eyes, freckles and a big smile. She is permanently in one scrape or another. Even her family seems rather on the crazy size. There's her mum, her stepfather, Terry, her eight-year-old twin half-brothers, her two much older stepbrothers, and her much younger half-brother and sister. Complicated, isn't it? They don't *all* live together. Luce just lives with her mum, her stepdad and her twin brothers.

Jaimini Riva (pronounced *Jay-m-nee Reever*) is Luce's best friend. Her family background is much simpler because she's an only child, though her mum is pregnant now, which Jaimini is over the moon about. Jaimini is the brainy one. It takes someone brainy to keep Luce under control at times. Jaimini's dad is black and her mum white, which means that Jaimini has got very dark skin, black eyes and long, silky black hair. Right now, I'm not sure where Jaimini is. She may be tucked up sensibly behind Luce, or she may be in the loo. I think half the boat is throwing up in some loo or other. I only hope I can last out the journey.

I don't know where Fen is, either. Fen, short for Fenella Brooks, is the ambitious one who started our Cafe Club going. Fen's Aunt Jan is the manageress of a cafe in Cableden, where we all live and go to school. We're all thirteen, so we couldn't get jobs, yet we were desperate to earn some money. It was Fen who came up with the fantastic idea of approaching her aunt to see if we could work at her cafe, taking it in turns so that we each did only one day from Monday to Saturday. We have a rota so that a different person gets to do Saturday each week, because the hours are longer. From Monday to Friday we only work for two hours after school. Fen, by the way, has got shoulder-length brown hair and a very determined look on her face. She's really strong, Fen is, and I don't mean just physically, although she *is* very good at sport and dance. PE is *my* favourite subject at school, so Fen and I have quite a lot in common. Fen's got two sisters, Rachel who's nine, and Emmy who's five.

The last member of the Cafe Club is Tash, short for Natasha Johnston, the peacemaker. Tash has quite short, dark hair, twinkling brown eyes and a lovely smile. She hates arguments and falling out. Her parents used to argue a lot, but now they're divorced and Tash doesn't see her dad any more. She lives with her mum, her older brother, Danny, and her little sister, Peta. I don't know where Tash is right now, either.

Smash! There goes another batch of crockery. The ferry company must be losing an awful lot of money. When the boat tips to one side, it feels as though the top deck must be practically in the sea, and when you look out of the other side, you can only see the side of the boat. No sky, no sea. I wish the captain would put out another announcement. I just feel like being reassured that we *are* going to be all right.

"Going to be sick."

That was Leah.

"Do you want me to help you to the loo?" I offered, bending down to see how she looked. Awful.

"Bag. Quick."

I thrust one of the pile of brown sick bags I had on the table at her in the nick of time. Poor old Leah. This was the fifth time she'd been sick.

Jaimini

Hi! It's Jaimini talking. I wish I knew where the others were. This boat trip is the worst I've ever suffered. I only woke up a few minutes ago, and though I'm feeling better than I was, I feel far from well. I've used up all my strength on lugging the dead weight of Lucy Edmunson out of the way of the passengers who are able to walk. I don't think there are many of those around at the moment, but all the same, Luce looked so untidy, limbs sticking out everywhere. She moaned and groaned a lot as I moved her, but didn't even bother to open her eyes to see what was happening, and I didn't have the strength to give her a running commentary on my struggle. Now that she's safely curled up in a corner I'm going to try and find the others. The trouble is, I don't want to investigate the loos, because I suspect they might be in a disgusting state. On the other hand, if one of my friends is alone in a loo, then I ought to go and check that they're all right. On the *other* hand (which makes it sound as though we all have three hands, I know), if one of my friends *is* in the loo, they probably want to be left in peace. I don't think I'd want company if I was being sick. Right, decision made. I'll head for the reclining-seats area.

Walking around in a boat that's violently tipping and lurching is practically impossible. You have to hold on to something with every step you take, but unfortunately that's not always possible. I mean, you can't hold on to a wall, you can only lean against it. But if the boat is tipping away from the wall at that moment, it's not much use. In the end – don't laugh – I crawled along. If I'd been crawling alone, in the normal course of events, people would have stared at me and thought I was madder than Luce, but because everybody's total attention was taken up with concentrating on personal survival, I didn't attract any funny looks at all. Crawling upstairs was surprisingly easy and I headed straight for the reclining-seats area.

"Jaimini, whatever have you done?"

"Hi, Fen. Are you OK?"

"Just about. I've been sick in the loo once and I feel OK now, but I'm not risking moving about. The trouble is, I don't know where Tash is, or Leah and Andy. But Jaimini, why on earth are you crawling like that?"

"It's the only way you can get about on this boat. I've left Luce fast asleep just outside the cafeteria, but I feel wide awake and I wanted to find you others."

"I'm sure Andy and Leah are together somewhere. Andy doesn't get seasick and she'll be looking after Leah, but I'm worried about Tash. I haven't seen her for ages, only I daren't move, because it's only the fact that I'm sitting still like that that's stopping me from being sick, I'm sure."

"I'll go and find her for you, don't worry. Just stay here and I'll come back as soon as I have any luck."

"Thanks, Jaimes. You're a star."

*   *   *

Luce

Hi! It's Luce speaking, the manically depressed, horribly ill, completely immobile one. OK, so I'm exaggerating a little. Maybe I'm still just the crazy one, but listen God, I promise I'll give up all my stupid habits, all my impulsive behaviour, I'll even become a nun if you want, anything, if you'll just do me a favour and take away this awful seasickness. I really can't cope a minute longer.

I know Jaimini thought I was asleep all that time, but I wasn't. You see, I can't even escape this terrible feeling by sleeping, like most people can. I just have to lie there in agony. I haven't even got the strength to go to the loo. Maybe I could ask Jaimini to go for me.

"Jaimini? Jaimini?" Where *is* that girl? Oh great! Now I'm not only in torment, but I'm in torment on my own. I'm going to find her. . . No, I'm not. I'm going to die. Oh, God!

Fen

Hi! It's Fen speaking.

I know Jaimini told me to stay here, but it's no good. I'm worried about Tash and I won't relax until I know she's OK. You see, Tash has got a secret that only *I* know about. She's an epileptic. That means that something happens in her brain that can trigger off a fit. Because she's not got the severe form of epilepsy, the fits she has are called absences. It's like she tunes out for about a minute and when she comes round again, she's no idea what's

7

been happening during that minute. It could be just a few seconds, even. Her eyes completely glaze over and her face goes slack. It's quite frightening to watch. Tash hardly ever has absences these days because her condition is controlled by medication, but I know it's a fear of hers that people won't like her when they find out about her epilepsy, and I promised I would always be there for her if by chance she had an absence in public. That's why I've got to find her now.

It didn't take me long to realize that Jaimini was right. There was only one possible way of getting round this boat, and that was on my hands and knees. I decided to head off in the opposite direction from Jaimini, though, on the grounds that it was silly for both of us to be looking in the same places. I hadn't got very far when the captain's voice came over the tannoy.

"This is Captain Harris speaking. I'm sorry that this is such a bad crossing for many of you, but I wanted to reassure you that the boat *is* perfectly safe, and to tell you that we are now through the worst of the weather. We hit a particularly nasty squall about twenty minutes ago, and from now on things can only get better, as they say. The wind speed has dropped to force six, and should continue to drop for the rest of the voyage."

I could hear the optimism in the captain's voice and it cheered me up. I hoped the others were all listening and feeling the same. I still had to find Tash, though. I stood up and found that I could walk around after all. My sick feeling hadn't gone, but it was nothing like as bad as it had been a few minutes before. I scanned all the lines of reclining seats and came out of the room to find myself more or less at the back of the boat. I went downstairs and into the duty-free shop and straight out again. Not a single passenger was buying duty-frees, and the girl at the till looked rather green around the gills, I thought. I looked in the other little shop but it was the same again, nobody there, except another pale-looking girl at the till.

There was no sign of Tash in either of the ladies' toilets on this deck, and I checked properly by calling out, "Tash, are you there?" each time. Three of the loos in the first one I went into were occupied, and when I called, "Tash!" no one replied. In the other, all of the loos were occupied, and instead of calling out I made absolutely sure by waiting for all six loos to vacate. No luck.

Next I headed for the self-service cafeteria and found that Jaimini had met up with Andy and Leah. Poor Leah was fast asleep under one of the tables. Well, I say "poor" Leah, but I suppose that being asleep is the best possible way to escape the awfulness of seasickness. The other three of us began whispering so as not to wake her.

"I'm worried about Tash," I began. Then, not wanting to sound too dramatic, in case the others started questioning why I should be any more worried about Tash than, say, Leah, I added, "I haven't seen her for ages."

"Do you want me to help you look?" Andy immediately offered. "Leah'll be fine now. The boat's definitely not rocking as much as before, and she can't possibly be sick again because there can't be anything left inside her."

So Andy, Jaimini and I all set off in search of Tash. We set about it very methodically, taking one deck each. Jaimini took the bottom deck, the one above the car deck. That was the easiest to search because it was largely cabins, and Tash couldn't be in a cabin as we hadn't booked any. I took the top deck and Andy took the one we were on, the middle one. The plan was to meet up in ten minutes in the cafeteria.

Leah

Hi. It's Leah speaking.

This has been the journey from hell. I woke up five minutes ago to find that fortunately I've managed to miss most of it by being asleep. I'll never forget the way I felt each time I woke up, though. Poor Andy has seen me at my very worst now. I'm really worried that she won't like me after this. I've been sick at least five times and I haven't had the energy to get to the loo so I've had to use those nasty brown bags. I'm going now, though, because I want to wash my face and wash out my mouth. When I woke up to find that Andy wasn't there, I was immediately anxious and upset. She obviously couldn't stand being near me for a second longer and I don't blame her. The problem is, I badly need Andy's friendship at this moment in time. I mean I always need it, of course, but now more than ever, because the six of us are going to stay with our penfriends in France.

Not long ago, we all had our penfriends staying with us at Cableden, but mine turned out to be a really horrible girl called Aline. The trouble was, I didn't realize how sly and manipulative she was until the very end of their stay. I can't bear to think of those days, because I was so horrible to Andy. I hadn't meant to be, but Aline sort of made me. No, I can't pin all the blame on her. I acted very weakly and I was ashamed of myself, but anyway, to

10

cut a long story short, by the time the French lot were due to go back, I hated Aline more than I'd ever hated anyone, and she said she never ever wanted to set eyes on me again. I made it quite clear that the feeling was mutual.

It's holiday time at the moment and this isn't a trip organized by the school or anything, it's entirely organized by us. You see, we were due to do the return trip with the rest of year eight at school, but there was a huge epidemic of a nasty virus going around at the time, and in the end there weren't enough people who were well enough to go, so the school's return visit had to be cancelled. Andy's penfriend, Laurette, came up with the brilliant idea of us six all going out together to make up for the big disappointment, so that's what we're doing. We've got one whole week away.

The arrangement is as follows: Andy and I are staying at the house of a boy called Jacques, who is almost like a boyfriend to Andy. To be perfectly honest, I'm not sure if he's a boyfriend or just a really really good friend. You see, when the French kids were staying in England, Andy and Jacques struck up this amazing relationship. They spent most of the ten-day visit hating each other's guts because of a whole series of misunderstandings, then, at the eleventh hour, they suddenly realized that they really liked each other. Of course, because Andy is bilingual, she speaks French as well as she speaks English. The rest of us all struggled along with the language barrier and made the best of it we could. Jaimini probably made the most successful attempts because she's so clever. Personally, I was terrible, I'm sure.

Anyway, back to the arrangements. Andy's penfriend, Laurette, who's really nice, and also very close to Andy, is going to stay at Jacques's place too, so that she doesn't miss out on seeing as much as possible of Andy. I'm also staying there, because, of course, I was left penfriend-less (if there is such a word) by Aline. Unfortunately, Aline is still going to be around, and I suppose it'll be hard to avoid seeing her. I feel really nervous about that. Jaimini is staying with her penfriend, Emma, and Luce is staying there too. Typically, Luce had chosen a boy for a pen-friend, called Benoît, but she regretted that decision when she met him, because he was computer-mad and not at all what Luce had had in mind for a penfriend! Tash and Fen are both staying with their penfriends. Tash's is called Celine, and Fen's is called Sophie. In under an hour's time we'll all be meeting up at the port. I can't help feeling excited, although, being me, I probably feel more worried than anything. I really want to find Andy to check she still likes me.

I sat up slowly to see how I felt. So far so good. Heaving myself up on to one of the seats I saw that there were now quite a few more people in the cafe. The place was still closed, though. I had been vaguely aware of crashing, smashing crockery and glass penetrating my dreams as I slept, so I guessed that they wouldn't be able to reopen for the rest of the journey. I sat still for a few minutes because I didn't want to rush anything. I was scared of that awful feeling coming back. Looking out of the boat, though, I could see that the sea was much calmer. The skies were still grey, but it wasn't that sheet rain falling any more, just a mild drizzle. The boat was tipping from side to side, but nothing like as badly as it had been doing before.

After a few moments I cautiously rose from my seat and walked a few steps. No problem. I felt a sudden rush of happiness that the nightmare seemed to be over. I sped up and nearly fell over Luce as I left the cafe. Her eyes stared up at me as though I was a ghost.

"Luce. Are you OK?"

"I can't answer. I'm dead."

"It's not half so choppy now. Why don't you try standing up? I've been as sick as anything, but I feel better now."

"I've told you, I'm dead."

"Come on, Luce. I'll help you."

Once she was on her feet, Luce's colour seemed to come flooding back and her freckles didn't look quite so obvious through her paleness. "You're right. I feel fine. Let's go and find the others," she said with a grin, as she set off briskly. I was glad she was back on form again.

We met Jaimini in no time at all. She'd been off searching for Tash along with Andy and Fen.

"Searching for Tash? Why all the fuss?" asked Luce. "She's probably throwing up in a loo somewhere and doesn't want to be searched for, thank you very much."

"Fen was worried," replied Jaimini, which obviously satisfied Luce because she shut up after that.

At that moment Fen appeared from the upper deck. "Any luck?" she asked Jaimini, without finding out how Luce or I were.

Jaimini shook her head.

"Yes, we're very well, thank you for caring so much," Luce informed Fen sarcastically.

"I can see that," Fen answered. "But I haven't seen Tash for about two hours, and I'm worried."

"We'll help you look," I offered, beginning to feel the stirrings of unease in case anything serious had happened to Tash.

"Have you looked in all the loos?" asked Luce.

"No, we never thought of that," replied Fen sarcastically.

"I was only trying to help," protested Luce, and that's when Andy appeared, looking very grim-faced.

"You OK?" she grinned, when she saw me.

I nodded. "Thanks for looking after me, Andy. It can't have been much fun."

She didn't even answer, she was so preoccupied with Tash. "I think it's time to notify someone official," she said a moment later. "Have you seen what's outside?"

"What?" we all asked.

"France. We'll be disembarking soon."

And just as though someone had heard her speak, over the tannoy came the voice of one of the crew. "Will all car and coach passengers please rejoin their vehicles. You are reminded that smoking is not allowed on the car decks, and we ask you kindly not to switch on your engine until your line of traffic is moving."

"It'll be foot passengers next," Fen said, and we all heard the note of panic in her voice. Poor Tash. Where *was* she?

Chapter 2

Tash

Hi! It's Tash speaking, and I'm in a terrible state because I've done a really stupid thing. Maybe one day I'll be able to laugh about it, but right now, I feel like dying with embarrassment. You see, I'm stuck in the men's toilets. What happened was, I felt violently sick about two hours ago and went rushing off to the loo. Fen was asleep at the time. I must have been so blindingly sure I was about to throw up all over the floor that I just dived into the first loo I saw. I never even noticed whether the picture on the door was of a man or a woman. The only thing on my mind was to get to the loo in time, and *that* I achieved. I'd been sick, then I was sick again and again, and then I straightened up and felt absolutely fine. I was about to open the door to the main area of the loos when I heard a voice. *That's a very deep voice for a woman*, I thought, then I heard another deep voice and a laugh, and it was then that I realized what I'd done.

There was no way I was going to walk brazenly out of the loo in front of two men. They were probably using the urinals. How absolutely, mortifyingly embarrassing! I'd just have to wait until there was silence, then make a dash for it. The trouble was that before those two men went out, another one came in, and so it continued. There then followed an endless stream of men coming in and out of those loos for the whole journey.

My heart was beating wildly the entire time because I felt sure that someone would realize that the end loo had been occupied for an awfully long time, but maybe men and boys are less observant than women and girls, because although the door handle rattled several times as people tried to open it, no one actually challenged me by calling out, "Come on, you're taking your time, mate, aren't you?" or whatever men would be likely to say to each other. I could imagine that would be the kind of thing that my brother, Danny, would call out, anyway. Oh, Danny! I wish you were here.

As time went on I started to get in a greater and greater state of alarm because I knew Leah would be worried, and I suspected that Fen would, too. If only I could get a message to them to say that I was all right, and I'd be out as soon as I could. I even considered pretending I was a boy with long hair, but I'm no actress, not like Luce, and I knew I'd never have the guts to stroll out like a boy. Everyone would stare at me and suspect me of being a pervert or something. I wished I had Andy's courage, then I could just face the music without worrying about it. I knew the kind of thing Andy would say if anyone challenged her: "Look, it was the men's loos or sick all over the floor, OK?"

Finally, immediately after the announcement about car

and coach passengers rejoining their vehicles, there was not a voice to be heard. I knew I had to get out quickly before I changed my mind, or before anyone else came in, so I pulled back the bolt and then *did* a bolt. I kept my head down all the way to the cafeteria, then I looked up and wondered where to find the others. As I did so my eyes met Fen's and she came plunging through the hordes of car and coach passengers, banging their duty-free bags against their legs in her hurry to get to me. We gave each other the biggest hug in the world.

"I've been so worried," she said. "Are you all right?"

I knew exactly what she meant. She thought I might have had a fit. I quickly reassured her that I was fine and by that time, the others had managed to fight their way through the oncoming crowds and, of course, all five of them wanted to know what on earth had happened to me. There was no way I could tell a lie. I knew they would have searched every inch of the boat. I took a deep breath.

"I was stuck in the men's loos."

After a ten-second silence it was Luce who cracked up first, but the others followed suit almost immediately and Fen, with her arm draped round my shoulder, said, "Tash, you've got to laugh. That is the funniest thing I've heard for a long time."

"I can't laugh yet," I said, with a smile.

"I'm not surprised," said Leah, who'd hardly produced more than a giggle. "It must have been awful for you. I would have worried myself sick."

"I'm sick of sick," said Luce. "Let's talk about something else."

"Would all foot passengers please disembark now via the gangway situated on C deck," came the announcement over the tannoy.

"We're here! We're here!" Luce said, jumping up and down, and I must admit, her excitement wore off on to me and made me forget the last two hours.

I had a picture of Celine in my mind, and as soon as we'd come down the stairs and were heading towards the terminal I began to look out for her. She's got shortish fair hair and very light coloured eyebrows. She's a bit smaller than me and a tiny bit younger. In fact, she's going to have her thirteenth birthday during this coming week. Glancing sideways at the others I saw that they were all doing the same thing – bobbing their heads from side to side to try and be the first to catch sight of a familiar face.

In the end it was Andy who recognized someone first, but she didn't say a word. All we knew was that one minute Andy was right beside us and the next she'd gone plunging forwards at a hundred miles an hour straight into the arms of Jacques, who's tall and blond. He spun her round and round and I smiled as she laughed up at him, looking so happy. The moment he put her down, she turned round and was face to face with Laurette. They both shrieked with delight at the sight of each other then gave each other four kisses and a hug. Remember, the French are very into kissing, and in this area we knew that they did four at a time.

I spotted Sophie, Fen's penfriend, at the same time as Fen did, and watched as Fen ran forward, then hung back at the last minute. She and Sophie did the four kisses much more shyly and sort of formally. By this time, the rest of the French party had joined the others. Jacques, Laurette and Sophie had obviously gone rushing on ahead to get there first. Jaimini's penfriend, Emma, and her mum were standing smiling at us all, and Emma introduced Jaimini and Luce to her mum. The kissing seemed to take forever this time because there were four people involved, which added up to thirty-two kisses in all! But where was Celine?

Then I saw her. She was dragging her mother along by the hand, but when she spotted me, she pulled away and gave me a big hug and no kisses. I felt very touched because she'd chosen to make me feel at home by giving me the English sort of greeting and not the French sort. Laurette's mum then came rushing up and Laurette introduced her to all of us, but she just shook our hands and gave us all very warm smiles.

So that was the welcome party complete. There were three mothers to do the driving, and next we had to decide whose cars we were all going in. In the end Andy went with Laurette, her mum, Jacques and Leah, I went with Celine, her mum, Fen and Sophie, and Luce and Jaimini went with Emma and her mum. The three cars travelled in convoy for the hour-and-a-half journey and I thought how different it must have been in our car and the car with Emma and her mum, compared to the car with Andy and Laurette and the others. For the hundredth time I found myself really envying Andy for being able to speak fluent French and communicate so easily. Fen and I had to make a huge effort and concentrate really hard to understand what Celine's mum was saying.

"Do you speak English?" I asked Madame Leblanc (Celine's mum) in French.

"Verrrry bad," she answered, grinning at me through the driving mirror. "So only French zeees week, *d'accord*?"

"*D'accord*," I replied, thinking how much improvement I was going to make. In one way it was good to be staying in a family on my own, like Fen was, too, but in another way I envied the others because at least they'd got one other English person with them. I didn't know how the week was planned, and whether or not we'd be doing lots of things together in families. I didn't even know whether the French families all knew each other particularly well or what. Just because we six Cafe Club girls get on so well together, it didn't mean that our penfriends were also so close to each other.

When the car stopped I started to get out, but Madame Leblanc said that this was Sophie's house and she was dropping Fen off here. Fen started to get out of the car and both of us must suddenly have had the same thought at the same moment.

"When am I going to see you again?" Fen said.

"I haven't got your phone number or anything," I said, getting out, even though I probably wasn't supposed to. We both turned to Madame Leblanc and tried in our stilted French to ask what was happening the next day, and whether Fen and Sophie would be spending time with Celine and me. Madame Leblanc was on the point of answering when Sophie's mum appeared. She was smiling at Fen and gave her the usual four kisses, but I noticed she didn't even shake hands with Madame Leblanc and the two women scarcely looked at each other. I didn't read anything into this. I just concluded that that's how the French acted. There was so much to get used to. So many customs and so much culture to learn.

"Will we see Tash and Celine tomorrow?" Fen asked Madame Leroi (Sophie's mum) very hesitantly.

"I don't think so, not tomorrow," came the answer in French.

"Yes we will," said Sophie and Celine very softly at exactly the same time, which cheered me up a bit, and I saw the relief on Fen's face, too. We were here to have a good time, and it wouldn't be half as much fun if the six of us were separated. Fen and I quickly wrote each other's phone numbers on our hands and then I got back into the car.

As soon as we pulled off there was a rapid exchange in French between Celine and her mum. I couldn't follow what was being said at all, except that it sounded like an argument that they were both trying hard to conceal. Every so often Madame Leblanc's voice rose, then quickly lowered again as though she was remembering that there was a visitor in the car. When we rolled into their drive I began to relax a little. It was a really pretty house with ivy growing up it. There were shutters on all the windows and the garden was a blaze of colour. A little hairy black dog came rushing out to greet us, followed by three small children and one slightly bigger one.

"Only those are mine," said Madame Leblanc with a smile as she pointed to two of the children. At least, that's what I thought she said, but I couldn't tell which two she'd indicated as all four came over and gave me one kiss each.

"Only one kiss?" I said to Celine.

"Because they are small children," she replied. I was learning fast.

In we went, with my bag and rucksack. The house was medium-sized, and I was given a guided tour straight away. There were three bedrooms, one for Celine and me, one for her parents, and one for her two little sisters. I was to sleep on a put-up bed in Celine's room. Celine was in a really bouncy, happy mood, and so were her two little sisters. The other two children appeared to have left. I quickly unpacked my things, then Celine said we were going to have something called a *gouter*, pronounced *goo-tay*. I didn't know what on earth that was, but it turned out to be a couple of slices of bread covered thickly with chocolate spread, and a mug of hot chocolate – only the mug was actually more like a bowl.

While we were eating, Celine told me with great excitement about her forthcoming birthday party. I had to keep stopping her and making her slow down because I couldn't understand a single word when she gabbled on. In the end, I gathered (if I understood correctly) that Celine was having a big party for fifty people, including grown-ups, mainly her relatives, who seemed to be coming from far and wide. The party was to take place on Saturday in the village hall and there would be a special catering firm coming in to serve the meal. Then there'd be a disco, games and songs.

I wanted to check that at least one of my English friends would be there, but I felt it was rude to ask straight out just like that, so I decided to leave it a while to see if I could work round to this question in a casual way later on. It would have been impossible for me to have asked about that just then anyway, because Celine had launched into her next piece of exciting news. Tomorrow, we were going out for the whole day and taking a picnic with us! We were going to a monkey reserve I think, though I may well have got that wrong, then we were going on to a chateau and to a forest. I felt very flattered that all this had been arranged in my honour, but I was dying to ask if I was going to see Fen or any of the others. We'd somehow left each other at the port, gone off in separate cars, and not really said anything about when we were going to meet again. I was happy with Celine, but I knew I'd have been much happier if I'd known that I was going to see the others every so often.

At seven o'clock in the evening I met Monsieur Leblanc, who seemed very nice. He had a tired, frazzled look, as though people had been pelting him with questions and phone calls all day long. He dropped a tatty-looking briefcase in the hall and his wife introduced him to me. I bet he wished that he could just kick off his shoes and flop into a chair with a glass of wine, and instead he had to be pleasant to this newly arrived English girl. I don't know where I found the vocab, but I managed to construct the following sentence in French, which I came out with as I was shaking hands with him.

"You look so tired, I don't mind if you ignore me for a while." I was quite proud of myself for saying this in French, and though I'd never dream of saying such a thing to an English man, it seemed OK in French.

After I'd spoken there was a sort of shocked silence and for a ghastly moment I thought I'd committed some kind of dreadful social gaffe, but then suddenly the whole family cracked up and Madame Leblanc laughed until the tears poured down her face.

"You Eenglish are verrry good," she managed to splutter as she laughed.

"I wouldn't dream of ignoring you," said Monsieur Leblanc in perfect English, with only his accent to show that he was French. I was shocked because, for some reason, I'd just assumed that he wouldn't speak any English. When I'd finished blushing I managed to laugh with them all.

The evening meal was fantastic. We talked a mixture of the two languages and I felt as though I was doing really well. At least everybody kept telling me that! The two little girls, who were called Katrine and Victoria, were sweet. Katrine was seven and Victoria five. They seemed so grown up, eating everything the grown-ups ate and really seeming to enjoy it. It was amazing to see little girls like that using sharp knives to cut a wedge of Camembert, then popping it into their mouths on the end of the knife! I know Fen's mum would have been having kittens if Emmy had done that, but Celine's parents didn't bat an eyelid, and I thought how good it was the way the little French children were expected to sit with the rest of the family for the evening meal and eat just like the adults do.

Monsieur Leblanc insisted that I would love French wine. No amount of assuring him that I'd tasted it twice in England and I'd hated it both times did any good. He poured out a nice big glass and I tried to drink at least half of it. Because I wasn't used to alcohol it went straight to my head, and though I felt light-headed I also felt very happy and relaxed enough to ask whether Fen and Sophie could come on the picnic the following day. I'd tried to compose the sentence in French, but in the end I took the lazy way out and just asked Monsieur Leblanc in English. Immediately he shot a glance at his wife, then realizing that she hadn't understood what I'd said, he translated for her, and her whole face changed. She'd been smiling, but the smile just slid away and a very serious look took its place. She said something in rapid French to her husband, who sighed, then turned to me and said in slow English: "There is a problem. The family of Sophie and our family are not friendly. Not at all. We are sorry because this is bad for you, I'm afraid."

I could tell he was embarrassed, because his English had gone to pot compared with the way he'd been speaking it up until then.

"But surely that doesn't affect the children, does it?" I asked, before I had time to check with myself whether this question was a bit impolite.

"Affect?"

"Affect, yes. I mean, surely the children are friendly, aren't they? Sophie and Celine are very friendly – I've seen them together."

"Hm. It is complicated. Maybe we make exception for this once." He turned to his wife and spoke in French, but I got the general drift. "Maybe just for once, as Natasha is with us, we should make an exception and take Sophie and her penfriend with us tomorrow?"

His wife just shrugged, then abruptly left the table, and at that moment the phone rang. It was Andy and Leah.

25

It was lovely to talk to them both. They were having a fantastic time. I was dying to tell them about the problem between Celine's family and Sophie's family, but I knew I had to be careful because the phone was in the same room as the table where we were all eating, and I knew by then that Monsieur Leblanc could speak good English. In the end I waited until there was plenty of noise at the table, then I lowered my voice and told them as quickly as possible about the great feud. Andy reassured me that she would make sure that we all got together, and that she was going to phone Fen straight after. Leah then said the same thing, and so I felt much better by the time I rang off.

When Madame Leblanc returned to the table, she was carrying an enormous gateau and was back to her normal smiley self. No more was said about the Leroi family, and the rest of the meal was as good as the first part had been, before I'd made my blundering request. It was only when Celine and I were getting ready for bed that I remembered something. In the funny mixture of French and English that we'd got used to using in England, we managed to have the following discussion.

"Sophie came in the car with your mother to collect us from the port. How is that different from going on a picnic?"

"She told her mother she was going with Laurette's mother. Otherwise her mother would not have let her come."

"But why, Celine? What *is* the problem between the two families?"

"It's too complicated to explain. Don't worry now. You will see Fen, but maybe not tomorrow."

Just before I went to sleep I remembered that I hadn't phoned Mum. I would phone her the next day. She told me that I could phone her whenever I wanted. She said she promised not to worry about me, and that she just hoped I would have a really good time. That was typical of Mum. She's the best mother in the world.

Chapter 3

Andy

It's rare that out of the six of us, I feel the most excited about anything. It's usually Luce or Fen. But I think that as we got off the boat and my eyes began to scan the port, I felt more excited than all the others. Then, when I saw Jacques, I wanted to burst. I'd thought about him so much since I'd said goodbye to him in England weeks before, and no matter how much you try to remember someone, the memory always fades and you start wondering, after a while, whether you're going to be disappointed when you see the person again. That's why it was like a double thrill when I first set eyes on Jacques again. He was exactly as I'd remember him, and I just ran into his arms, which isn't like me at all.

Then there was Laurette, which made everything even better. Laurette and I got really close when she stayed with me in England, and seeing her again at the port in France, it felt as though we'd only said goodbye the day before.

All the way to Jacques's place we reminisced about everything that had happened in England. I sat in the back with Jacques and Leah, and Laurette sat in the front, with her mum driving. Laurette's mum seemed really easy to get on with. She immediately told us to call her Therese, and all the time we were gabbling on in French she kept interrupting and telling me to translate for Leah. She obviously felt sorry for Leah, who could only understand very little at the speed we were talking.

Jacques explained to me that the reason his mum hadn't come to collect us was because she thought the house looked a mess and she wanted to get it tidied up before our arrival. I felt very honoured to think that someone was specially tidying their house for Leah and me.

"Our house is far too little for all of you," said Therese, "but Gaston and I hope to see a lot of you during your stay, and we'd like to meet the rest of the Cafe Club properly, too."

"I've told Mum loads about you all," said Laurette, to explain how her mum knew about the existence of our Cafe Club. "Mum's been trying to organize a day when all the French families and you six English girls can get together."

"It'll probably be at our place because we've got a big garden," said Jacques, "and Dad loves entertaining."

"Your *dad* loves entertaining?"

"Yes, it's Dad who does all the cooking. Mum's not that domesticated."

I was dying to meet Jacques's family. He'd already told me that he has one brother, who's ten.

When we got to Jacques's place, Leah and I both gasped. It was like a castle. It was, in fact, a small chateau, and I could see that the grounds were going to go on for ever. Jacques's mum came rushing out to meet us. She was the complete opposite to my mum. She was wearing tight, faded jeans with holes in them, and a cotton top. She'd got long hair, which she'd loosely tied back and fixed with a big silver clip. She wore nothing on her feet, very little make-up, no jewellery apart from an anklet, and she looked really lovely – not exactly good-looking, but very attractive. She put her hands on my shoulders as she kissed me and she broke off after each of the four kisses to look at me and say something. So it went like this:

Kiss.

"It's so lovely to meet you at last."

Kiss.

"Jacques has told me so much about you."

Kiss.

"You're just as I'd imagined you would be."

Kiss.

"And this is Leah," I quickly said, because I was feeling more and more sorry for Leah. I seemed to be getting a hero's welcome, while poor Leah was being left in the background. But I needn't have worried. Madame de Vallois was launching into her next round of kisses.

Kiss.

"Leah, my dear."

Kiss.

"Welcome to our home."

Kiss.

"It's so lovely to have two such charming English girls staying with us."

Kiss.

"Mum, she doesn't understand a word you're saying."

"Oh, I thought you spoke French. Sorry," said Jacques's mum to Leah, in French.

"I told you, Mum, it's Andy who speaks French."

"But you know me, Jacques. I'm so forgetful. Now, my dears, you must call me Marie-Jo. It's short for Marie-Joseph, but I find that a touch religious, so I'm known as Marie-Jo, OK?" Marie-Joe suddenly realized that Laurette's mum was standing there holding one of our bags. "Therese, my dear, how are you?" Two kisses. "Let me take this bag, and everybody must come and have aperitifs. It's a little early, but who cares! We are celebrating, aren't we?" She turned her big warm smile on Leah and me, then gave Laurette a kiss, before handing the bag to Jacques and telling him to take Leah's bag, too, which he did without a murmur. This left Marie-Jo free to put an arm round Leah and one round me, and it was like this that we entered her vast house. She reminded me of a sort of modern-day fairy godmother who went round spreading happiness everywhere she went.

From the moment we stepped inside her conservatory, or sun lounge, or whatever that breathtaking room was supposed to be, I felt as though I was in a palace. Leah and I kept on looking at each other, eyes enormous. She was obviously as filled with awe as I was. Jacques looked embarrassed every time I said how amazing it all was. Marie-Jo looked delighted with our reactions, as though she personally had designed and built the place. The more interest we showed, the more she went into detail about the structure of the building. It was becoming obvious that Marie-Jo, who had given the impression of being very scatty, actually knew a thing or two about building and design. She made it quite clear that she hadn't made any curtains or done any decorating, but when we came to a beautiful fireplace, she said she had built that.

The house was vast. Laurette, Leah and I could all have had separate bedrooms if we'd wanted. Marie-Jo gave us the choice, but we chose to sleep in the same room, which had three double beds in it! Jacques's bedroom was on another floor, and that was also huge. His little brother Bastien's room was next door to ours and was only a bit smaller. Then there were at least three other bedrooms. One of the bedrooms had a plaque on its closed door, which said "*Chambre de Lisa*" (Lisa's bedroom).

"Who's Lisa?" I asked Jacques.

"The *nourrice*," he replied. "She's away at the moment."

I had the impression he was about to add something but changed his mind. I didn't press it, but I was surprised that he'd never before mentioned that they had a child-minder. I didn't think that Marie-Jo worked, so surely it was an incredible luxury to have someone living in to help with the children, especially as Jacques was fourteen.

The attic had been converted into a huge games room, and we'd already been told that there were two studies.

"This is *my* study," said Marie-Jo, opening the door briefly. "Very boring to look at," she added, wrinkling her nose. On the walls were masses of pinboards covered with photos of buildings and A4 sheets of complicated designs. At one end of the room was a huge drawing board with a massive sheet of very thick, glossy tracing paper stretched over it. There were rulers and set squares and compasses and rubbers and sharp pencils beside the draw-ing board. Something was slowly dawning on me.

"Mum's an architect," Jacques said softly, which proved my theory correct.

"She's an architect," I whispered to Leah.

"I though she'd be something high-powered," Leah whispered back, and it struck me, not for the first time, how perceptive Leah is, or maybe she'd just got a bigger imagination than me. Now I knew why they needed Lisa to look after Bastien. But I was wondering something else by then. I wasn't sure whether to ask about it. In the end I whispered to Jacques.

"Your mum didn't design *this* house, did she?"

Jacques nodded, and I gasped and quickly told Leah, who also gasped. Marie-Jo must be a genius. She'd made the house look like a modern-day castle, with turrets and things. I don't know who was responsible for the garden and its design, but it was as impressive and grand as the house, and even had a swimming pool in the secluded part that was out of the wind.

We didn't meet Monsieur de Vallois until the evening, although it turned out that he'd been in his study all the time. I asked Jacques what his father's job was, and Jacques smiled and replied that his dad was an architect, too.

"Serge. You must call me Serge. Monsieur de Vallois makes me feel ancient."

Serge looked like the last man in the world that I could have imagined Marie-Jo being married to. He was very neat and tidy and ordinary-looking, and he seemed quite a bit younger than Marie-Jo.

"Do you want a *Pastis*, Serge?" Jacques asked his father,

as we sat round the table on the verandah, and something else clicked in my brain just then. This must be Jacques's stepdad. How strange that Jacques had never mentioned before that he lived with his mum and his stepdad. I noticed that Bastien called Serge "Papa" though. I thought I'd ask Laurette about this at some point.

We'd already had one lot of *aperitifs* (sort of nibbles, really) with Laurette and Therese, and when Therese had gone we played table tennis and darts in the attic. The teams were Jacques and me against Laurette and Leah. Jacques and I won. Then we went outside and played frisbee on one of the lawns.

"This is so luxurious, isn't it?" Leah said, looking ecstatic. "I won't want to go home after this."

I'd been having the same thought, but not for the same reasons. I knew I was going to find it a terrible wrench to leave Jacques for the second time. It would be bad enough leaving Laurette, but it would be far worse leaving Jacques. We had a funny relationship. I couldn't tell if it was boyfriend and girlfriend, or just good friends. We hugged each other, we sat close to each other, we wanted to be with each other all the time, but we didn't hold hands or anything like that. I'd often wondered what Jacques thought about it, and whether he wanted it to be a proper "going out" with each other. I didn't think so. In the end I'd decided to stop analyzing and just be happy with what I'd got.

After the *aperitifs* it was time for dinner, but Marie-Jo more or less ordered Leah and me to go and phone all our friends and our parents. "They will want to be sure that you're safe," she insisted, when we said it was all right, we didn't have to phone England, because it would be so expensive. "No problem, *cherie*. Just phone them to make me happy, all right?" So we did. I left Leah on her own while she was talking to her mum, so I've no idea what she was saying, then I quickly phoned my mum and told her that I'd save all my news till we got home, but that we'd arrived safely, the house was a modern chateau, Jacques's parents were lovely, and we were having a great time. Then I phoned Jaimini and Luce.

It was Emma who answered the phone and she sounded very bubbly. I could hear Luce giggling in the background. She came on the phone a moment later and talked at about a hundred miles per hour about what a great time she and Jaimini were having, and about these adorable puppies that she was already planning on smuggling back into England. Jaimini and Leah had a chat with each other, then I phoned Tash and heard about the family feud between Celine's parents and Sophie's. Tash was worried that the bad feeling between the two families might prevent her from seeing much of Fen during the week, so I told her not to worry and that I would be contacting Fen any minute. By the time Leah had said more or less the same thing, I think Tash was feeling better. Next we tried to get hold of Fen but there was no reply, and although we tried later on, there was still no reply from the Lerois'.

I was starving, and the dinner that Serge had cooked was absolutely delicious. Marie-Jo poured the wine and the drinks for us, so it was a real role reversal. Laurette was staying at Jacques's for most of our visit, so that she and I could see as much as possible of each other, and it was lovely to have her at dinner too. She was making a big effort to talk in English with Leah. It was really nice of Jacques's parents to let her stay as well, because they didn't seem to know her any better than they knew us two. Jacques and Laurette didn't even go to the same school, so they really only knew each other vaguely.

Jacques had wine to drink and Laurette had half a glass, but Leah and I didn't want it so we had lemonade along with Bastien. Bastien was a very shy boy who spent a lot of time on his own in his room, drawing and painting. He asked if he could go and draw halfway through the meal, and Marie-Jo said she didn't mind as long as her guests had no objection. I said jokingly that he could go only if he promised to show me what he'd drawn, but I must have said the wrong thing because Bastien blushed and said he'd stay at the table after all.

"Only Lisa ever gets to see his pictures," Jacques explained to me.

"When is Lisa coming back, Maman?"

"Soon, *cheri*. In a day or two."

Bastien looked so upset that I thought the best thing he could do would be to get on with his drawing.

"I was only joking, Bastien. Of course we don't mind if you go," I quickly told him and he got up quietly and left the table, still looking rather pink.

"So haven't you *ever* seen any of Bastien's pictures?" I asked the rest of the family.

"I once saw one," Serge said, "but only because I happened to be in his room when he'd left his sketch pad open one day. It was a picture of a woman that he'd drawn. At least, I thought it was a woman. I didn't ask about it because Bastien's such a private person that you have to wait till he offers information."

"Serge gets through to him more easily than Mum does, though, don't you, Serge?" Jacques asked.

Serge shrugged modestly, but Marie-Jo agreed with Jacques.

"And what about Lisa? Is she on holiday?" asked Leah, who was gaining confidence in French all the time, as Marie-Jo and Serge really congratulated her every time she uttered a French word.

"We're not sure," said Marie-Jo hesitantly. "Lisa suddenly announced that she was going away and that she would be away for a few days. She didn't ask permission, she merely informed us of her decision. Nor did she tell us where she was going or why. So we're in the dark, I'm afraid. We just hope that she's safe and not in any kind of trouble."

I thought Marie-Jo was being incredibly fair-minded about the whole thing. I was sure that most adults would be furious under the circumstances.

"How old is she?" asked Laurette.

"Eighteen. She's an adult, of course, but I still worry," said Marie-Jo.

I translated everything for Leah, who then asked when Lisa actually went.

"This morning," said Marie-Jo.

"Tell her I hope it wasn't anything to do with us two coming," Leah said to me.

"No, no, no," replied Marie-Jo when I'd translated. "She's a funny girl. I could tell she had something on her mind, but I didn't want to interfere with her private life.

I didn't feel it was my business. And then, of course, there's the fact that she's English."

"English?"

"Yes, sorry, didn't we say?"

Neither Leah nor I had imagined that Lisa would be anything other than French, so it came as quite a shock to us. I felt curious about her instantly, and hoped she'd come back very soon.

That night, Leah, Laurette and I were very excited about going to bed in such a magnificent bedroom. We were determined to stay awake for ages and talk to each other, but in no time at all the other two were fast asleep. I didn't mind. I was happy to lie in the darkness and think back through the whole day, especially the moment when Jacques and I had met each other at the port. I was just drifting off to sleep with this lovely thought in my mind when I heard a sudden loud noise, like something being dropped in the room above. I tried to recall the layout of the house, and as far as I could remember, it was Lisa's room above the one that we were in. But Lisa was away, so had someone else gone into her room? I listened and listened for any other sounds from above, but there were none. Then I couldn't get to sleep for ages, because I was trying to work out if that room *was* the one above ours.

I looked at my watch and saw that it was half past midnight, so I decided to risk creeping upstairs to see if I was right about Lisa's room. I opened the door without a sound, shut it behind me and tiptoed down the passage. There was no light on our floor, but I could just about see from the light that was coming down the stairs at the end of the passage. I crept up the stairs and walked along the landing above until I judged that I was directly above our room. I was right. It *was* Lisa's room. I looked to right and left. Nobody was about. I pressed my ear to the door but couldn't hear a thing.

An idea had entered my head and I was desperately trying to pretend that it hadn't, because my trouble is, the moment I've considered a possible line of action, however way out or unwise it would be to take that action, I *have* to do it. There's something inside me that makes me go ahead with things, and sometimes I have to work like mad on manufacturing the courage to do them. This was one of those times, because it had crossed my mind that I could let myself into the room, then, if someone was in there, I could pretend I'd been to the loo and got lost, or I was mixed up about which room I was supposed to be in.

My heart beating wildly on the silent landing, I slowly turned the door handle. The door was locked.

Chapter 4

Jaimini

Luce is keeping me in stitches. I don't think I've ever seen her throw herself into anything quite so wholeheartedly as she is doing at the moment. You should hear her talking French. It's almost as though she wants to make sure she uses every French word she's ever learnt at every opportunity. For example, when Madame Cardin, Emma's mum, who is really nice, asked us if we wanted a drink, Luce said in French, "I would very much like a drink, thank you. It is so kind of you to offer me a drink. What is the choice of drinks, please?" I saw Madame Cardin smile and look slightly taken aback, and since then the poor lady has been wearing a sort of semi-bewildered expression, as though she's not sure whether to classify Luce as totally mad, slightly eccentric, charmingly English or rather naughty because she's secretly taking the mickey.

Actually, I envy Luce, because she hasn't got any inhibitions about speaking the language. By the end of our stay, she will certainly have learnt more than me, because I'm quite shy about using my French.

Emma has got an older sister called Michelle. She's

sixteen and is very petite and very shy indeed. It's all worked out really well, because Emma is much more light-hearted than her sister, so Luce and she go well together, and Michelle and I go well together, too. She's very keen on English and keeps asking me lots of questions.

When we first arrived at the house I felt really tired, but after a quick guided tour (it's only a little house, but very modern, quite like ours, in fact), we went into the garden and played with their beautiful puppies. Their dog has just had six. Two of them have gone to new homes, but the other four are still waiting. Luce rootled to the bottom of her vocab to describe the puppies and came out with: "Oh, they're so beautiful and sweet and brilliant and marvellous and terrific and pretty and charming and I love them."

Michelle met my eyes and we both cracked up, to Luce's irritation. "You should try exercising your French a bit more, Jaimes," she told me, so I dutifully asked how old they were, and which one was born first, and what breed the father was. Luce then said, "What's that in English, Jaimini? I said, 'Try exercising your French,' not 'Try outshining the world's best linguists.'" Michelle must have been very good at English because she understood what Luce had said, and she burst out laughing.

Although the Cardins' house was quite small, their garden was big, and they had a little orchard at the back that didn't belong to them, but that they were allowed to go into. We knew it was quite a kiddish thing to do, but we all had a brilliant game of *cache-cache*, which is the French for hide-and-seek, then we taught Emma and Michelle forty-forty, which is a really good variation on the game. At one point while I was counting to a hundred, my mind started wandering, and I wondered how the others were getting on and when we'd all meet up. We hadn't really thought ahead when we'd driven off in three different cars. I hoped Fen and Tash were OK because they were separated. And I hoped Leah was all right, because Andy had got Jacques *and* Laurette, whereas Leah didn't really have anyone. I was sure Andy wouldn't let her get left out, though.

Monsieur Cardin was rather a distant sort of man. He was perfectly pleasant, but always looked preoccupied and hardly spoke at all. Maybe he was shy, like Michelle. Apart from Emma, they were a very quiet family altogether, and even Emma went quiet when her father was around. I expect they didn't know what had hit them when Luce turned up like a tornado, full of life and French vocab!

During the evening meal it was arranged that we should go to the beach the next day. Luce and I were really excited, but all the same I wanted to be sure that we were going to meet up with the others at some point during the week. Madame Cardin said she knew Celine's family and Laurette's family quite well, but she didn't really know the others, though she saw no reason why all of the English and French penfriends shouldn't get together. It was great to have Michelle, whose English was so good, to help with the translating, because Madame Cardin spoke very little English, and Monsieur Cardin spoke practically none. When we were tucking into slices of apple and cherry pie, the phone rang, and it was Andy and Leah. It was lovely to chat to them, and Andy was trying to organize for us all to get together. I felt better knowing that it was in her capable hands. She and Leah were having a great time, too. Apparently Jacques's place was a chateau, and his parents were absolutely wonderful.

The next morning we all woke up early and full of excitement. Luce and I had been sleeping on a double mattress on the floor. Luce had wriggled around all night but insisted that she had never moved a muscle in her sleep. Michelle came into our room before breakfast and we all sat round and chatted and played music for about an hour. It was so lovely the way Michelle joined in with us, just as though she was thirteen, too. I found myself liking her more and more. She did a fantastic French plait on my hair, but funnily enough the French call them *tresses africaines* or African plaits.

"I wonder if they call them English plaits in Africa?" Luce mused as she applied bright-green nail varnish to her toe nails.

Breakfast was the most huge meal, even though it's the English who have the reputation for eating the biggest breakfasts. Luce ate more than anyone, but with almost every other mouthful she told us how fat she was going to be by the end of the week, then amused the Cardin family with an imitation of a very fat person who could hardly walk trying to sit down in a chair, then trying to get up again. Monsieur Cardin – the quiet one – actually let out the smallest of laughs at her performance, and murmured in French that she was "*terrible*". When I'd talked with Michelle about this she explained that it means something different in French. Far from being a bad thing, the word *terrible* means excellent. Good old Luce.

Monsieur Cardin is a chiropodist. He'd been unemployed for quite a while and had decided to retrain in chiropody. He was in the middle of his training but had already got one or two patients, if I understood Michelle correctly. He was due to see these two patients the following day, but not till the evening, so he decided to come with us to the beach. Madame Cardin looked as though she was going to faint with amazement, and Michelle whispered to me that normally they couldn't get their dad to go anywhere with them. Emma was just staring at her dad as though he'd sprouted horns.

It took half an hour in the car to get to the beach and we sang loudly all the way. The songs we sang were a mixture of French and English, and in the end we actually composed a song that included both languages. Monsieur Cardin was the only one who didn't sing, but I could see through the driving mirror that he was smiling. The beach was the loveliest beach I'd ever seen. I've only ever been to the beach two or three times in my life. We've always gone on holiday to places in the country, or to cities. The sand was beautiful and golden and stretched as far as we could see in both directions. There were very few people on the beach and the sea was quite far in, but on its way out. It was altogether perfect.

I helped Monsieur and Madame Cardin and Michelle to set out all the towels and mats and the windbreak, while Luce and Emma peeled off their clothes and ran off to the sea in their swimsuits, which turned out to be practically identical, to their intense amusement. About ten seconds later Luce came rushing back like a cat escaping a water pistol and said that the sea was freezing, but she'd managed to get her big toe wet. Monsieur Cardin sat on one of those foldaway plastic beach chairs and took out his newspaper.

Madame Cardin lay down on her stomach and got Michelle to cover her with sun-protection cream. I did the same for Michelle, and everybody said how lucky I was having such dark skin. I must admit, this is the one time I really appreciate my skin. Luce took off down to the sea again and I decided to go with her this time. She grabbed my hand and said we were going to enter the sea by the "torture method", which meant as slowly as possible.

Emma was already swimming around and insisting that it was wonderful once you got used to it. Luce asked me to translate and I said, "She said, 'Watch out for jellyfish and sharks.'" Luce's scream pierced through the roar of the waves, and it wasn't till I laughed and told her I was only mucking about that she would agree to come in the sea. I couldn't wait any longer for her, so I went plunging in, then swam about frantically to get warm. Emma was right. It was lovely once you were used to it. Luce spent the next twenty minutes getting in up to her shoulders. "Don't you think you're taking the 'torture method' a little too far?" I joked with her, but she couldn't even manage a witty retort because she was concentrating on overcoming the cold with every fibre of her body.

The Cardins had packed very lightweight surfboards and Emma sent Luce off to get them. We only managed to translate surfboards in mime, and I still couldn't be sure that Luce and I had understood correctly. When Luce returned, Michelle was with her and they were carrying two surfboards each. Michelle said her parents were both asleep, and added that it was good for her father to relax like this. I didn't ask why, but I felt curious. We then had a wonderful half hour in the sea, off and on the boards – more off than on in Luce's case.

The next hour was spent burying Luce in the sand on her instructions. When we'd done it, she insisted on showing Emma and Michelle's parents, and also on having her photo taken for posterity. I told her not to bother Monsieur and Madame Cardin, who were enjoying the peace, but Emma went off to get her parents. She came back with her father. She was holding his hand, I noticed, and she seemed really happy to have him with her. He walked quite slowly, and folded his arms to look at Luce, with his head on one side, as though he were surveying a piece of fine art. Then he turned to Michelle and said something that I understood to be, "How about burying Emma now, then the rest of us can go out to lunch, while these two stay here!"

Michelle and Emma seemed over-the-top delighted that he'd cracked a joke, and I realized that he obviously wasn't normally a very jokey sort of person. Madame Cardin had packed a lovely picnic, which we all tucked into, then the grown-ups went off for a walk and we four did a bit of sunbathing. I plastered Luce with high-factor sun-protection cream. It was too hot and sticky after a bit so we put two sunshades up and played cards, only they kept blowing away and we had to give up in the end.

When Monsieur and Madame Cardin came back from their walk we all played a game of *boules* together. We used proper French bowls, which are silver and very heavy. You hold them with your palm down and throw them, rather than roll them. It was great fun, even though both Luce and I were absolutely useless at it. Monsieur Cardin was excellent at it, and Michelle told me that he used to play in lots of *boules* competitions before his. . . She stopped her sentence there and moved on to something else, but again, she had made me curious.

We left the beach in the middle of the afternoon and went on to look round a sweet little town further along the coast. Luce and I bought postcards and wrote them in a little cafe, where we drank Coke.

"Let's pay for the drinks," I suggested to Luce, and she immediately started fishing round in her purse in a totally unsubtle way.

"No, no, *we* pay," said Monsieur Cardin.

"We would like to pay, please," I said politely, and after a bit of arguing, they let us pay.

"Are you enjoying yourselves?" Madame Cardin asked us, and Luce and I both assured her that we were having the time of our lives, which we were. "What would you like to do tomorrow?" she then asked. I really wanted to see the rest of the Cafe Club, but I thought it might be rather rude to suggest it. It might give the impression that we hadn't really enjoyed today because of the others not being there, which wasn't true, of course. In fact, I could honestly say that the day was one of the best of my life.

"Would it be possible to see our friends?" Luce asked, and Madame Cardin said, "Yes, of course. We must phone them. Of course you want to see your friends."

"But today *has* been really brilliant," I assured her.

"I know, my dear," she said, patting my hand.

Monsieur Cardin didn't make any contribution to this conversation, maybe because he knew he'd be working the next day.

At home in the evening we played with the puppies again and took loads of photos, then had another nice meal, and finally, Emma, Luce and I sat round the telephone while Madame Cardin tried to get hold of the other families. First she tried Laurette's mother, whom I gathered she knew the best.

It was impossible to follow most of what she was saying, but when she'd finished talking she told us that Jacques's mum was already trying to organize a get-together for everyone, and that she would be phoning us later to sort it out. So we all played a card game called *Uno*, which was brilliant fun, and after about half an hour the phone rang. Sure enough, it was Jacques's mum. I could tell from Madame Cardin's tone of voice that she didn't know Madame de Vallois all that well. She sounded more formal than usual, and she smiled a lot and nodded, even though Madame de Vallois obviously couldn't see her. (Body language is amazing, isn't it?)

"Well," she said, as she replaced the phone and began to speak very slowly and carefully for Luce's and my benefit, "Madame de Vallois thinks the best solution is for everyone to meet at her house tomorrow. She will leave you all to spend the day as you want, and when the parents come at the end of the day to collect you, we can discuss an outing for all the families. Madame de Vallois mentioned Disneyland, Paris!"

Well, you can imagine the effect that that had on Luce and me. Even Emma, who'd been there before, couldn't contain her excitement.

"Disneyland! Yes! Mega!" said Luce, and the three of us went mad, dancing round the room like five-year-olds. When we were in the middle of these crazy antics, Monsieur Cardin came into the room, and Emma immediately stopped dancing and chanting, so I naturally followed suit, but Luce, who must have felt completely at home, carried on. Then she shocked us all by having the nerve to dance her way up to Monsieur Cardin and start waltzing him round the room as though she'd known him all her life. I saw Madame Cardin's eyes widen in alarm, and it suddenly struck me that maybe Monsieur Cardin had a heart problem or something like that, and that had been what Michelle had been about to say earlier on. "He used to play in lots of *boules* competitions before his *heart-bypass operation.*"

Omigod! And here was Luce, careering with him round the room. Emma looked very worried indeed and I told Luce to stop, which she did, suddenly turning pink as though she'd just woken up from being hypnotized, and realized she'd been doing something very foolish indeed.

"What a girl!" said Monsieur Cardin, shaking his head. "Are you always so – ?"

He didn't know what word to use, so I decided to help him out. "Crazy?"

"Yes, crazy – *folle*," he said, but he was smiling as he went back out again, and Emma and her mum exchanged silent, gobsmacked looks, as though they'd just witnessed Monsieur Cardin taking off and flying through the window. Something interesting was happening here, but I didn't feel as though we knew the family well enough to ask what it was. Maybe I'd discreetly ask Michelle later.

As it happened I had the perfect chance because Emma and Luce both fell asleep in front of the television, and

Michelle and I weren't tired at all, as we went up to her room and she showed me her photograph album and talked about boyfriends. She didn't have a boyfriend, but there was someone she really wanted to go out with, only he didn't seem to notice her, let alone ask her out. I sympathized, but didn't know what else to say about that. I thought the boy must be mad because Michelle was so pretty. In a way she was like an older version of Andy, only her hair was long and fine.

"I hope Luce isn't too loud and crazy for your father," I ventured tentatively.

"No, quite the opposite. It's a funny thing, but I think she's the best medicine he's ever had."

"Medicine? Oh, dear. Is he ill?"

"I try to tell you in Engleesh," said Michelle. "He had, how you say, nervous breakdown two year ago, and he never return to himself – his real self. Maman say his nerves are fragile. You understand what I want to say?" I nodded. "So always now, for a very long time, we walk on tiptoe very softly when he is near, and we don't ask him to do things or to come places, because the answer is always 'No'. The only theeng he do well is his work, because he is so pleased to have thees new training for job. That was why he had the breakdown – because he worked too hard in his job and then lost his job. You understand?"

"I understand," I said, feeling very sorry for the whole family and trying to imagine what it must be like to live in such an atmosphere. "It must be difficult for you all."

"Yes, I think so. But today, we don't believe what we hear, when he say, 'Yes, I come to the beach also.' It is a miracle, and it is, I think, because of Lucy. You must not tell her thees. It is very important that she don't know at all, because I theenk if we had been more normal and less moving quietly and talking quietly in our family, Papa would have got better much sooner. Eet is best that Lucy continues to be natural with Papa. You understand?"

"Yes, I understand completely, and I won't say a word to Luce, but you must warn Emma not to say anything, either."

"I do that already. She know."

"Good old Luce," I thought, as I lay beside her later in our bed on the floor. "Without realizing it, you're outwitting the French medical profession!" I smiled to myself in the dark.

Chapter 5

Fen

It was a weird boat journey, everybody being separated, then all the worry of losing Tash, and finally France appearing without any warning – then Tash herself appearing without any warning. It was strange meeting Sophie, too. When we first saw each other it was great, but then neither of us knew what to do. As we went along in the car I found myself envying Andy and Leah who were going to be together, and also Jaimini and Luce, for the same reason.

Madame Leblanc, Celine's mum, dropped Sophie and me off and hardly exchanged two words with Madame Leroi, Sophie's mum. I think that was probably the moment that I first realized that there was some sort of problem between the two families. Tash and I had quickly exchanged phone numbers and then the car had disappeared. Madame Leroi was very nice and welcoming to me. She was most concerned in case I hadn't eaten enough on the boat. She spoke a bit of English and I managed to make her realize that the boat journey had been awful. She made lots of sympathetic noises and asked me if I wanted to have a little rest. I said I would love something to eat, because I did suddenly feel starving hungry.

Sophie said very little throughout all this, and I wondered whether she was always so quiet. It was true that in England she had probably been the quietest of all the French penfriends, but I had put that down to shyness, and thought that she would be relaxed and noisier on home ground.

While we were eating *tartines*, which are slices of French loaf spread thickly with whatever you want but usually something sweet (I had strawberry jam), Sophie's brother came in. There was something about him I didn't like, but I wasn't sure what it was. Maybe it was the fact that his eyes never quite met mine. He looked sort of shifty. Sophie introduced me to him. She said he was called Thibault, which you pronounce *Teebo*. She'd told me that she had a sixteen-year-old brother, but I'd forgotten what his name was. Thibault was wearing a black T-shirt and blue jeans. He also wore a very fine silver chain round his neck. Lots of boys would look stupid wearing a necklace, but not Thibault. It kind of went with his image. When he spoke to me he still wasn't bothering to look at me.

"Good crossing?" (At least, that's what I think he was asking.)

"No, horrible," I replied in English, then Sophie took over and told him all about the voyage as I had tried to describe it in my stuttery French in the car.

"You like France?" Thibault then asked me in English, and I thought what a ridiculous question that was. How could I judge so quickly? I'd been to France a few times before on day trips, so I tried to say that I liked it so far.

While I was in the middle of composing a sentence about that, Thibault interrupted me and asked me which part of England I came from. Without even bothering to hear my reply, he immediately said that he didn't like England. He'd been there once to stay with his penfriend, and as far as I could gather, he thought the food was awful, the family he stayed with were horrible and the place was ugly. There's not a lot you can say to that when you don't speak the language, and it was making me really frustrated that I couldn't come back at Thibault and tell him how narrow-minded I thought he was.

I'd never realized before, but I'm obviously quite patriotic. I mean, I never knew my country meant anything to me, but hearing Thibault rubbishing England like that made me so angry. All I wanted to do was escape from this family for a little while and go and bury myself in a French textbook so that I could learn as much as possible as quickly as possible, then I'd be able to argue on the same level with the great Thibault, who made me sick. He even had the cheek to say that the English played rubbish football and didn't know how to dress. I understood that all right, because of his over-the-top miming.

Madame Leroi laughed lightly and said, "Don't go on about it, Thibault," or something that I think translated roughly like that. Goodness knows why she didn't tell her son to stop being so rude to their English visitor, but she didn't. I had had enough of Mr France-Appreciation-Society by then, and though I didn't know anything about the football and I couldn't really comment on the food or the fashion because they were a matter of taste (and I just sensed that I'd get nowhere arguing about those things), there was one thing that I knew I *could* get him on, and that was pop music.

"Do you like pop music?" I asked Thibault.

He shrugged and said something that could have been a yes, so I then quoted English group after English band after English singer, and said, "Do you like them?" each time. Every time he conceded that he did like them, and every time I said "English" before going on to the next one. I was so deeply determined to score some points over this obnoxious brother of Sophie's that I didn't even notice how Sophie or her mother were taking my onslaught. When I paused for breath after naming about ten groups, I glanced at Madame Leroi and noticed that she had stopped washing up and clearing away, and was leaning against the sink, following the conversation with a look of amusement on her face. And that's when another boy of about the same age as Thibault came into the kitchen, looking as though he owned the place. Surely Sophie hadn't got two brothers, had she? I was sure she'd only mentioned one. This second boy must be a friend of the first one, so why did he seem to be treating the place as though he lived there, then?

"This is my brother, Nicholas," said Sophie. "This is Fen, from England."

Uh-oh! Wrong! I had just been laying into a friend of the family. No wonder Madame Leroi had done no more than to tell Thibault to ease off a bit.

"Did you have a good crossing?" asked Nicholas very slowly in French, while shaking my hand.

"It was very windy," I managed to reply in French, using a completely different tone of voice from the one that I'd used to address Thibault.

Madame Leroi then filled Nicholas in on the famous boat crossing, and Thibault announced that he would see us later. He didn't waste any time saying goodbye, just vanished. As soon as he'd gone, Madame Leroi told me that I'd been brilliant, because in her opinion, Thibault was a very bad-mannered boy. Nicholas wanted to know what had happened, and he laughed like mad when his mother and sister told him.

"Thibault and I are going to the cinema later. Do you want to come too?" Nicholas asked Sophie and me. I was praying that Sophie would say no, or otherwise say that it was up to me, but she did neither. Instead she looked totally made up with the idea and said we'd love to come. Madame Leroi hadn't been paying attention and just beamed at everybody when Sophie told her later that we were all going out to the cinema together. She added that she was pleased because her husband was going out with friends that evening and now she could join him.

I had a room to myself, and I was left to unpack and get changed. This took me no time at all, so I sat and stared out of the window and wondered what the others would all be doing. I expected Luce and Jaimini would be having a great time because they'd got each other. Andy and Leah would definitely be having a great time because of Andy getting on so well with Jacques and Laurette, as well as speaking French. But what about Tash? She was on her own, like me. Maybe I'd give her a call.

I asked Madame Leroi if it would be all right for me to give Tash a call at Celine's. Madame Leroi tried to smile, but I could tell it was forced, and said why didn't I leave it till a bit later, because after all, I'd scarcely arrived. It was a slightly odd reply, I thought, and it got me thinking, so I went off to find Sophie, who was in the garden. In my poor French I tried to discover from her if there was some sort of problem between her family and the Leblancs. Then, in the slowest, most basic French she could muster, Sophie patiently explained to me what had happened between the families. I had to stop her lots of times and ask her to repeat things, or to say them more slowly, or in different words, but I think I understood correctly by the end.

Apparently, two years ago, the Leblancs asked Nicholas to babysit Celine's two little sisters, Katrine and Victoria. Nicholas stayed the night there because the parents were so late coming home, then in the morning he biked back home. At lunchtime there was a phone call from Monsieur Leblanc saying that three of their videos had gone missing and that he didn't mind Nicholas taking them, but he wished he'd asked permission. Not only had three videos disappeared, but also some money. Nicholas didn't know what on earth Monsieur Leblanc was talking about. He insisted that he hadn't even seen those videos among their collection, and that he wouldn't have dreamt of taking videos without asking permission first, but Monsieur Leblanc was adamant, and he even insulted Madame Leroi by saying that she had brought her son up to be a thief and a liar.

That made Monsieur Leroi get involved and he told Monsieur Leblanc that he had no right to make false accusations like that. Then there was a huge bust-up, and since then, the only contact between the two families had been between Celine and Sophie. They don't ever talk about the rift between the families, but they're both very tense if they are together with either of their mothers. They're *never* together with either of their fathers, but Celine's mum is not as bitter as Madame Leroi. Apparently, Madame Leroi would never have driven Celine and Sophie in the same car from the port, for example. That's why Madame Leblanc did it. And that's why it may be quite difficult for me to see Tash this week.

This story of Sophie's shocked me, but what I didn't like was what she said at the end of it.

"Surely it doesn't matter that you and Tash do not meet each other for one little week? You see her all the time in England? No? And you're here to visit me? No?"

She smiled, and I tried to smile back and say something that was supposed to mean "Yes, of course," but my heart wasn't in it, and I was feeling more and more depressed with every passing minute. I knew what I would do. I would get Andy to sort it out. I would phone Andy and tell her the whole story. No, I couldn't, could I, because we were supposed to be going to the cinema with the charming Thibault. Right, I'd somehow survive the evening and then I'd get hold of Andy the following day, come what may. And maybe the film would turn out to be a really good one and I'd have a great evening after all.

At six-thirty, Monsieur Leroi turned up. He didn't seem to be in a particularly good mood. Perhaps he wasn't too impressed about coming home to a visitor who couldn't speak the language. It was almost a relief when seven o'clock came and the three of us went out. We were walking to the cinema and meeting Thibault there. As we strolled through the town, I wished we could just carry on walking around. It was such a pretty town and the evening sky was a deep orangey-red, shooting bits of its light through the trees and winking at us in the narrow gaps between the square white houses. Everywhere looked so clean and yet so soft. I didn't feel like sitting in a stuffy cinema at all.

I sat between Sophie and Thibault. Thibault chewed gum loudly all through the film and also laughed more loudly than anyone else in the cinema. He really fancied himself. I couldn't wait till the film finished because I hardly understood a word, and I had the feeling that even if I'd understood every single bit, I still wouldn't have liked it. While pretending to watch it avidly, I sat there in the dark going through all the great British films I knew, and planning on throwing a few into the conversation for Thibault's benefit later.

Thank goodness it wasn't a very long film, and afterwards Nicholas suggested that we all went to a local bar for a beer. I didn't know about the beer, but I liked the idea of the bar because there was always the chance that I might just come across one or more of the others. Anyway, I was keen to sample a typical French bar, which I knew was more like a cafe than a pub.

The moment we'd got through the door my depression returned, because this was just as dull and dingy as the cinema. Thibault went to the bar to get lemonades for Sophie and me, and beers for himself and Nicholas, while Nicholas went through to the far end of the bar and reserved the pool table. The two of them then started playing pool, without asking us if we wanted to join in.

So Sophie and I drank our lemonades and talked, but

I kept an eye on the door on the off-chance that one of the others might come in. The lemonade tasted revolting. It was very different from English lemonade – much more bitter. As we sat there, I realized that I was beginning to feel quite dizzy and strange. I saw Sophie press her fingers against her forehead, and wondered if she was feeling as bad as me, which was odd, because I thought my weird feeling was some sort of after-ferry effect.

At almost exactly the same time as each other, though, the two of us suddenly came to life. We began to talk much more and to giggle a lot. Somewhere in the back of my mind I knew I was behaving rather badly, but for some unknown reason I didn't care. When I spoke, it was as though my words didn't come from me. Weird! Everything seemed so hysterically funny all of a sudden. I noticed some people on the next table looking at us as if we were mad, and I found myself turning to them and saying, "What are you staring at?" because I knew they wouldn't understand. I didn't even know whether Sophie had understood what I'd just said, but she was leaning back in her chair and laughing like a hyena.

"Shall we sneak off and go back to your house on our own?" I said to Sophie a few minutes later. This seemed like a very wicked exciting plan. Sophie leant forwards and beckoned to me. I was only across the table, but I leant forwards too, so that our noses were nearly touching. then we both jumped back with a shriek because Thibault had plonked two more lemonades on the table for us.

"Merci bucket," I said, laughing hysterically at my wonderful wit. Actually I wasn't thirsty at all, but the lemonade didn't taste quite so bitter now I was used to it. "Cheers!" I said to Sophie in a loud voice, as I chinked my glass against hers a bit too forcefully. "Drink, quick!" I went on, because somewhere at the back of my mind was the idea that we had to get away.

Sophie grinned and said, "OK. Quick." Then we both gulped the entire contents of our glasses, before getting up to go.

My body felt most peculiar when I stood up. It was my legs. They didn't seem to be working properly. I was sure I was suffering from post-seasickness syndrome. Sophie started giggling uncontrollably and I couldn't remember what we'd been talking about that was amusing her so much, so I just giggled with her.

After that we couldn't be bothered to talk any more, so we sang as we staggered all the way home. My depression had completely gone and in its place was a lovely feeling that everything was right with the world. I thought it must be because we'd got away from Nicholas and Thibault, and it was nearly bedtime, and tomorrow I would be able to phone Andy.

"Let's play some music while Maman and Papa are out," suggested Sophie, when we were lying on the floor in the Lerois' sitting room. I thought that sounded like a good idea. We went through the pile of CDs and managed to drop the whole lot. Quite a few of them fell out of their cases, but as Sophie said, they were very tough and no damage was done. The only trouble was that Sophie pulled herself up by grabbing the top of the cupboard where they were kept, but she missed the cupboard and dragged the heavy cut-glass ashtray down, which smashed four of the CDs in one hit.

"Papa won't find out if we throw away the evidence," Sophie said, piling the broken CD pieces up, one on top of the other. "He never listens to CDs. I bet he doesn't even know what's in here." Goodness knows if that's what she said, or just what I *thought* she said, but I didn't really care anyway.

We eventually found some music that we both liked and I taught Sophie an English disco dance, but for some reason or other, my legs were still suffering from that post-seasickness thing and Sophie seemed to have caught it from me, so we kept banging into things.

"I know, let's have some of Papa's port," said Sophie, grinning wickedly. I nodded excitedly because I just felt like a drink, and it would be cool to try some alcohol. I *did* think the measures that Sophie poured were a bit big, though.

"Are you sure your dad won't notice?" I tried to ask her. This made her realize how much she'd poured out, so she attempted to pour it back into the bottle again, but she was making a right mess of it, and it was going all over the carpet.

"Give it here," I said. "I'll do it." I didn't seem to be able to pour any better than Sophie could, which was unusual for me, because I was normally a very good pourer indeed. And it was while I was in the middle of trying to get more in the bottle than on the carpet that the door to the living room opened and in walked Monsieur and Madame Leroi. Madame Leroi looked very pretty, I thought, because I hadn't seen her all dressed up before, so I told her so in my best French.

"*Tres tres tres chic!*" I said, congratulating myself on

remembering the word *chic*. For some reason or other she didn't look very pleased about my compliment. Maybe I'd used the wrong word after all. I tried to think of another word, but couldn't, so decided to butter up Monsieur instead.

"*Belle soiree?*" I asked, smiling like mad, and again congratulating myself for choosing such a very French expression, but he, too, looked pretty serious. In fact, come to think about it, they both looked positively thundery. I hadn't the foggiest idea why, until I saw that Sophie had fallen asleep on the carpet.

"*Tres fatiguee,*" I commented, poking Sophie's leg.

The next thing I knew, I was being hauled to my feet by Madame Leroi, while Monsieur Leroi did the same with Sophie.

"*Au lit, jeune fille,*" she said to me. I could tell she was cross, but we'd only taken one little drink each and had hardly spilt any, and we'd left the broken CD pieces in a neat pile on the carpet. The French obviously flew off the handle more easily than the English. I'd soon cheer her up again.

"*Demain, chez Leblanc, voir Tash?*" I asked, as she helped me along to my bedroom. I'd still got those weak legs, you see. I was asking whether we could go to the Leblancs' to see Tash the next day.

"*Absolument pas!*" she replied. And then she said something in English about what I did in England, and how I had no right to act like that in her home. Everything was very hazy in my head, but somewhere at the back of my mind, something was trying to push its way through to tell me that the next day was going to be bad, *very* bad.

Even my head seemed to be suffering from post-seasickness trauma. I must have got that wrong. Everything would be fine the next day.

"*Bonne nuit, Madame. Merci pour –* " For what? I couldn't remember. In fact, if you want the truth, I couldn't remember where I was or who I was talking to. Never mind. The bed was lovely and soft.

Chapter 6

Luce

I really liked Emma's little house from the first moment I set eyes on it. We've got quite a big, rambling sort of house in England, and it's also quite old, so it made a nice change to be in a little modern house, like Jaimini's.

When we got there we went more or less straight into the garden and played with four of the most adorable puppies in the entire world. *Adorable!* That's another word. I think I impressed everyone with my massive French vocabulary. I know Jaimes is supposed to be the brainy one, but I reckon I've got the edge over her when it comes to the old lingo.

Madame Cardin is what I call ordinary. I don't mean that horribly or anything, but somehow I always get on best with people who are *out* of the ordinary. Take Andy's dad. Now he is the strictest man on earth, and all the rest of the Cafe Club, including his own daughter, I might add, are scared of him. But me? No. That's because he interests me with his hooded eyes and his sarcastic manner. Also, I think there must be something seriously wrong with him that he has to be so horrible and distant all the time. Anyway, I've noticed that the more light-hearted and jokey you are with Andy's dad, the better he seems to like it, almost as though he wants to be close to people but doesn't quite know how to go about it, so he relies on other people to do it for him.

I'm telling you all this because I reckon Monsieur Cardin is a bit the same. You didn't need a psychology degree to notice that the whole family was treating him as though he'd fall over and break if you dared to say "Boo". As soon as I realized this, I thought, *Aha! He's got "Andy's dad" syndrome, therefore he needs the same treatment*. So I set about it with a vengeance, and I can tell it's working already. Of course Jaimini, Emma and Michelle all think I'm just being my usual crazy, out-of-control self. Little do they know!

You should have seen their faces when I grabbed the unsuspecting Monsieur Cardin and waltzed him round the room. I knew he'd love it, and he did. He wants to relax, but he can't, as all the time everybody is treating him as though he's going for the Mr Fragile-of-the-Year Award (or should I say *Monsieur Fragile de l'Annee* Award?).

French beaches are absolutely, blissfully *chouette*! (That's a French word. It means brilliant.) If you say "sweat" with a *sh* instead of an *s* at the beginning, you've got the pronunciation. The sea, however, was glacial. How my big toe managed to remain attached to my foot when I dipped it in the icy water, I'll never know. Getting buried in the sand started off as a good idea, but I quickly became bored. I only suggested it in the first place as part of Monsieur Cardin's Luce-therapy, but in the end I was glad I did suffer the boredom. It was well worth it to get his reaction. He actually cracked a joke, and to see the look on the faces of the rest of the Cardins, you'd think he came from a planet where jokes hadn't been invented, and they were witnessing a miracle – a jokeless person joking.

In the afternoon, when we were writing postcards in a sweet little cafe (but not as sweet as *the* Cafe, of course!), Madame Cardin suddenly asked us what we wanted to do the next day. I'd been dying to see the others and to hear all about what adventures they were having, and to show off my wonderful French to Andy, so I said that that's what I'd like to do. I don't mean that I said all that. I just said I'd like to see the others, and Madame Cardin seemed to think that was a good idea.

After our second delicious evening meal *chez* Cardin, Emma, Jaimes and I sat round waiting to hear the verdict on the idea of a day spent with the others. While Madame Cardin talked to Laurette's mum, I lost myself in my thoughts about all that had happened so far. I felt very comfortable in this family. It had worked out brilliantly for me and Jaimes, because Emma's sister, Michelle, turned out to be very similar in character to Jaimes, while Emma, although nowhere near as impulsive and crazy as me, was a whole lot more like me than like Jaimini. Before breakfast, Michelle had been doing a French plait in Jaimini's hair and I'd managed to take a photo of them when their heads were close together. I'm dying to see how that photo turns out because I reckon it will be excellent, though I say it myself. They both looked so pretty and so happy.

Anyway, there was no verdict after that first phone call, because apparently Jacques's mum was organizing for us all to get together the following day, and sure enough, she phoned a bit later and it was decided that we would all go over there. I couldn't wait to see everyone. In fact, I was so excited I fell asleep in front of the television and had to be woken up by Jaimini to go to bed!

The following day I was first awake. I was on the point of waking the other two up when I decided that I'd do a bit of exploring on my own instead, so I quickly got dressed in jeans and a T-shirt and crept downstairs and out of the house. I was feeling pretty virtuous because I'd actually got myself organized for once and grabbed a ten-franc piece and also a bit of paper with the Cardins' phone number written on it. I wasn't planning on getting lost, but I knew how easily that kind of thing came to me, so I was all prepared! The house was very quiet, and no wonder – it was only half past seven.

I felt absolutely full of energy and completely right with the world, and it was blissful to walk down the calm, peaceful road with no traffic around. After I'd been walking for about twenty minutes or so, concentrating hard on keeping my bearings all the time because I was going more and more off the beaten track, I came across a farm. I stopped and stared into the yard behind the gate. There was something about this farm that was very different from English farms. It somehow had more character. I made a mental note to ask Monsieur Cardin about French farming at some point, but I think the difference was that this was a small farm with all the lovely little touches that you only find in children's story books.

When my twin brothers, Tim and Leo, were younger, I used to read to them from a book called *Tattlequack Farm*, and the place always looked so sweet and cosy. Well, that's what *this* farm reminded me of. I looked round for a name on the gate or the wall, but there wasn't one, so I christened it Tattlequack Farm and made another mental note to come back later in the week and take some photos to show to the twins when I got back. In the yard were three or four turkeys, a duck and five ducklings, a couple of guinea fowl and a few hens. They were all roaming around quacking and chattering. By the rabbit hutches slept an Alsatian. This was getting more and more like *Tattlequack Farm* every second. The dog in *that* story was an Alsatian, too. I decided I'd give this one the same name as the Tattlequack one.

"Major!" I called out in a cheerful voice.

Major woke up instantly, fixed me with his beady eye and did two loud barks, followed by a low, continuous growl. If he was anything like the dog in the book, he was just showing off. On the other hand, you never knew. He might be genuinely fierce. I looked round to see if there were any signs warning me about the ferocious guard dog, but I couldn't see any. There was one sign though. "*Oeufs – 20 francs la douzaine*". That meant, presumably, that you could buy half-a-dozen eggs for ten francs. Great! That was exactly what I'd got in my purse. I was determined to buy six eggs and give them to Madame Cardin as a present. I went to the front door of the farmhouse, which came right on to the road, and knocked. It was still only eight o'clock in the morning, but farmers were well known for getting up early, so I didn't worry that I'd be disturbing anyone.

When I'd knocked three times and still got no reply, I went back to the gate. Major was sitting right in the middle of the yard among the duck family and the turkeys and chickens. He wasn't growling any more, just watching. Behind him I could see haystacks and wood piles and two old-fashioned milking machines. Beyond that I could see cows in the fields, and also a small figure trudging along carrying a bucket or something. This must be the farmer, or maybe the farmer's wife. It was hard to tell at that distance. It didn't really matter. I just wanted someone to sell me the eggs. I took another look at Major and decided it was safe to risk entering the farm and walking as far as the milking machines, then attracting the farmer's attention.

As I opened the gate, Major didn't move a muscle. Surely he would have pounced on me by now if he meant trouble, I said to myself, but a part of me was a bit scared. "Don't show your fear," I told myself. Animals can sense fear and it makes them more dangerous. "Just act dead casual, Luce." I decided that it might be encouraging for Major if I spoke in his mother tongue, so as I inched forwards I said, "*Tres bien, mon grand chien, Majeur. Tres bien. Tres tres bien.*" I kept up this gentle patter all the way past him and he still didn't move a muscle. The trouble was that I was getting more and more scared. It had suddenly hit me that I must have been totally bonkers (so what's new?) to risk walking past a French Alsatian in a deserted farmyard. I'd been so carried away with the idea of this farm being like that nice safe story-book farm that I'd been blind to the dangers of a guard dog. I only just made it past Major without fainting, and the moment

I was the other side of him, he turned and watched me. As I didn't dare have my back to him, I walked backwards and prayed that I wouldn't fall over any turkeys or anything. I kept up the "*Tres bien*," patter, but my voice was shaking and I didn't think Major looked as though he would tolerate my going a single step further. A quick glance into the distance told me that even the farmer had deserted the place, so I decided to get out as fast as possible.

The moment I'd made this decision and started the torturously slow return journey past Major, whom I'd rechristened Snarl, I caught sight of a little table beside one of the haystacks where there were some eggs in a bowl. Perhaps the idea was that people helped themselves, but I couldn't see a little pot for the money. On the other hand, there were a couple of empty egg boxes underneath the table. Unfortunately, they were both large boxes for a dozen eggs, but that wouldn't have to matter.

"Just give me one more minute, Snarl, and I'll be out of your hair, all right?" I told the motionless, but totally alert dog, resorting to English and hoping he might enjoy the challenge of a second language. With a shaking hand I put my ten-franc piece on the table right next to the egg bowl, then I took six eggs, which left six in the bowl, and put them into the egg box, before heading back to the gate. It was tempting to make a dash for it, but I decided that slow and steady had worked up till now, so I'd stick to the same formula until I was safely on the other side of the gate. It only took about thirty seconds to get out, but those seconds seemed to go on for ever, and the relief when I got to the other side of the gate was enormous. Snarl was living up to his name and doing just that, so off I went, before anyone came up and asked me what I was doing marching off with a box of eggs.

I was so busy congratulating myself for escaping without injury or attracting attention to myself that I didn't notice where I was walking, and after a few minutes I realized that I'd done the very thing I'd been trying so hard not to do: get lost!

"Now *think*, Luce. Work backwards. Start at the farm."

But try as I might, I couldn't remember if and when I'd turned off since the farm. All the same, I had a rough idea of the direction I had to go in, so I headed off at a brisker pace and just hoped I'd recognize something fairly soon, because I didn't have the ten-franc piece now, did I? I followed the sound of the traffic, and soon came to the centre of the village. I knew the way home from here, because we'd come this way when we'd gone to the beach the previous day. Thank goodness for that. Only now there was another problem, because without any warning at all, the heavens had opened and it was bucketing down. I knew it was likely to be one of those very quick, very violent summer storms, but, all the same, if I stayed out in it a moment longer I'd be drenched.

Brilliant! A cafe, and open as well. It would be rare to find a cafe open in a little town like this in England at eight-twenty in the morning. I rushed inside and sat down at one of the tables. But I'd no sooner sat down than the waitress, a large woman in her fifties, was at my side. She did an up-and-down jerk of the head at me, which I took to mean "What can I get you to drink, Mademoiselle?" or probably more like "What d'you want then?"

Uh-oh. I couldn't even order a lemonade because I had no money. What was worse, I couldn't explain. I would have been able to manage to say, "No money," in French, but I didn't think that would exactly endear me to the woman, so I just stood up, smiled, shrugged, and pointed to the rain. She watched me as though I was a loony, and, in a burst of inspiration, I said, "English. Sorry. *Anglaise*."

Unfortunately there was still no change in the woman's expression, but I was saved by a comforting hand on the shoulder pushing me gently back into my chair. Talk about a knight in shining armour. Here was an extremely good-looking French boy of about fifteen or sixteen, who was smoothly telling the waitress that we would like two coffees. I don't like coffee, but I knew I was about to have a cup. I smiled at him and said, "*Merci*," and he came out with a string of French words from which I recognized one – "*rien*" – so I guess he was probably telling me to think nothing of it.

How I wished I was Andy at that moment, then I could really get talking to him, but as it was, all I could do was stare at his lovely black T-shirt and the fine silver chain around his neck.

"*Anglaise?*" he asked, even though we'd already established that.

"*Oui*," I replied.

"*Vacances?*" he asked.

"*Oui*," I replied.

"*Ici?*" he asked.

"*Oui*," I replied.

"*Mauvais temps*," he said, pointing to the rain outside. I knew "*mauvais temps*". It meant "bad weather". I couldn't keep saying "*oui*" all the time, though, so I tried to vary it a bit with "*Il pleut*", which means "it's raining". The moment the words were out of my mouth, I thought how utterly stupid they sounded. It was obvious to us both that it was raining, wasn't it? I decided I'd try my own question.

"*Vous, vacances?*"

"*Non.*" He then came out with another great long spiel that included the word "*travail*", so I took it he worked somewhere local, though I was surprised, because he didn't look old enough. After that we were stuck, but fortunately, the coffee came.

"*Comment tu t'appelles?*" he asked, when I'd managed to swallow two mouthfuls of the thick, black bitter concoction without grimacing.

This was better. I could cope with this. This was first-lesson French.

"*Je m'appelle Lucy*," I replied, and wondered why he was grinning. I realized immediately I should have just said "Lucy". After all, I wasn't in school now, was I?

"*Quel age as-tu?*" he then asked.

This was a tricky one. Should I say fourteen, or even fifteen? Yes, it would seem a whole lot more sophisticated.

"*J'ai quinze ans*," I told him, and watched him grin again. I could feel myself blushing, and wondered if he was grinning because I'd given him the schoolgirl answer, or because he guessed I was lying. Either way, it was pretty embarrassing.

He'd drunk his coffee, and at the sound of a horn tooting outside he suddenly stood up, plonked some coins on the table, gave me another quickfire sentence, of which there was not a single word I understood, then headed for the door.

"*Merci beaucoup*," I called out before he disappeared altogether, because though I was sure that every good knight-in-shining-armour story ended differently from this, at least he had got me out of a mess in the first place, and I was grateful to him for that. So I smiled at the still unsmiling waitress and set off back home. It was a pretty safe bet that Jaimini and the others would be up and about by then (it was ten to nine as I went round to the back of the house) and I couldn't wait to give Madame Cardin her present from Tattlequack Farm!

Chapter 7

Leah

For once, I think I can say I'm not worrying about anything. Oh no, I tell a lie. I'm worrying about Tash and Fen. I thought it was too good to be true. When we phoned Tash yesterday evening she told Andy and me about this feud between Celine's family and Sophie's family, where Fen is staying. Apparently, Celine's mum even hinted that Tash and Fen might not get to see each other during the week, but Andy reassured Tash on the phone that she would make sure they did. When I got on the phone I tried my best to tell Tash not to worry, because I had great faith in Andy's ability to sort it all out. After that I was dying to speak to Fen, but there was no reply. I hoped Fen was out enjoying herself somewhere. I felt so lucky to be in this wonderful house, or chateau, with such a lovely French family, *and* Laurette, *and* Andy.

Before we'd come to France I'd worried in case my horrible penfriend Aline was around, but now I'd been here one night I felt completely safe. It was seven-thirty in the morning and I was the only one out of us three awake. I wondered if Jacques was awake yet. The place was so huge you couldn't hear any noises unless they were directly above or below you. I got out of bed – a double one – and crept over to the curtains. It looked like a beautiful day. I left the curtains a fraction open so I could look out from my bed without too much light coming in and waking up the others. Then I lay there and thought about the previous day. It's funny how certain things stay in your mind more than others, and eventually only the really meaningful memories remain.

The first moment that really stuck in my memory from yesterday was being sick on that boat, the second was worrying about Tash being missing, the third was seeing Andy run into Jacques's arms and watching the happiness on both of their faces, and the next was being kissed by Marie-Jo. After that, if I had to choose one moment in this amazing chateau, it would be stepping into the conservatory, which was full of perfume and light. The plants and flowers were mainly either white or purple, and the two colours looked stunning together. I know it sounds a funny thing to say, but when I saw that conservatory I could imagine how it would sound if I played it on the piano. You see, I think of so much of life in musical terms, and if I find something really beautiful I imagine it in sound.

It didn't surprise me when Andy told me that Marie-Jo was an architect. I think it's great that someone can be so warm-hearted and scatty and yet so high-powered. Serge is really nice, too, and so is Bastien. I'd love to see his pictures, but it's unlikely that it will ever happen if he's not even shown his art to the rest of his family.

"Hi."

"Hi, Andy."

"Been awake long?"

"Ten minutes."

"Laurette awake?"

I looked over to her bed.

"Doesn't look like it."

"Guess what, Leah?" Andy then whispered, so that I could hardly hear her. Her eyes looked even bigger than usual, which made me think that whatever she was about to say must be very interesting.

"What?"

"Last night I heard a loud bang coming from the room above here. It was just as though someone had dropped something on to the floor, and I couldn't resist going upstairs to have a look."

"You went creeping round the house in the dead of night?" I shivered at the thought of it.

"No one was about, but when I got upstairs to the room that would be directly above this one, it was Lisa's."

"Lisa's?" I was trying to work out what all this meant. "But Lisa's away."

"Exactly. So it must have been someone else."

"But does that matter?" I couldn't see what all the intrigue was about. "Maybe Marie-Jo went in there for some reason or other."

"Like what?"

"Er, to change the bedding?"

"At half past twelve at night?"

"Is that what time it was?"

She nodded.

"Well, maybe something just happened to drop on to

the floor by itself. It needn't have been anything heavy. Things always sound heavier when you're in the room below."

"There's one thing I haven't told you yet, Leah." I waited. "I tried the door and it was locked."

"You tried the door? Are you totally crazy?"

"I just wanted to see if someone was in there."

"Maybe Jacques decided to swap bedrooms for the night, but he didn't want anyone to know, so he locked the door."

"And maybe the moon turned green during the night," replied Andy with a withering look.

"Are you going to tell him?"

"Jacques? Yes."

"What about Laurette?"

"Not yet. I'd rather wait and see what Jacques has to say. Also, I'm quite curious to see whether we have an extra person at the breakfast table. Maybe Lisa came back and slept in her room as usual, and locked the door as usual."

"Why lock the door?"

"Dunno, but I suppose some people do. I mean, you do when you're in a hotel, don't you?"

"S'pose so."

There were no unexplained extra people at the breakfast table and the breakfast was absolutely delicious. We ate warm croissants and warm *pain au chocolat* and drank hot chocolate. I was in heaven. Jacques challenged Andy to a game of table tennis, and they left the table before the rest of us. I guessed Andy would tell Jacques about the noise in the night while they were up in the attic on their own.

"Can I help you wash up?" I asked in my best French, and Marie-Jo put her arm round me and said I was very very kind, but that she could easily manage, what with husbands and dishwashers! At least, judging from the way she was grinning at Serge and patting the dishwasher, I guessed that was what she said. "Do you mind if I go into the garden?" I then asked.

"You must do whatever you want to do," Serge told me in English. "Please do not ask permission. Unless you want permission to set fire to the place or something of that nature," he twinkled, "there is no need to ask. *D'accord?*"

"*D'accord,*" I replied. So Laurette and I went off into the garden. As we left the kitchen Marie-Jo said something to Laurette that I half-understood, and which Laurette explained to me outside.

"Marie-Jo wants to know if you would like to go to the market at St Lomas this morning, then go to the beach this afternoon?"

"That would be brilliant!" I told her in my best French. Then I remembered Fen and Tash. "When do you think we'll get to see the others?"

"Marie-Jo is organizing a day here for everybody. She said the house and the garden will be open to the public – French and English all day tomorrow!"

Marie-Jo was such a sweet, thoughtful person. I began to idolize her at that moment. I decided that I ought to try and be like her. I should relax more, and worry less. I even considered having my hair cut to the same length as hers and seeing if I could get it to look a bit shaggier by layering it. Then I'd let my jeans get really tatty and holey and people would look at me and think I was totally cool. We had been walking along and I had been staring into space, having all these wonderful thoughts about my new image, when I suddenly focused on the garden and real life and thought, *in your dreams, Leah!*

"Which do you think is our bedroom window?" I asked Laurette, and after scanning the building for a moment, she pointed to one. The window above it was firmly closed, and all over the wall there was a beautiful vine. The house looked so beautiful that all thoughts of noises in the night seemed ridiculous, so Laurette and I went to have a look at the swimming pool, which even had a bar beside it!

The market was brilliant. I took quite a few photos, and Andy took loads of me and Laurette and Jacques, and of Marie-Jo, too. Serge didn't come with us. I think he was working at home. Bastien had gone out with a friend of his for the day.

There was a wonderful smell of sizzling onions, chips, hot dogs and kebabs that drifted all over the whole market, even though the food stalls were all at one end. The smell at the cheese stalls was enough to knock you out, and the fish stalls were even worse. I bought some cheese in little wooden boxes for Mum and Dad. Marie-Jo suggested which ones I should buy. Andy spent ages looking through hundreds of books, and in the end she bought two. They looked very thick and boring to me but Andy said that they were books of French poetry and that her parents would love them.

The stall with rings and bracelets and purses and neck-laces and things was my favourite. I wanted to take home something for Kim from this stall, and also something for myself. Andy and I decided to buy leather bracelets with our names sculpted into them. Someone was sculpting in the names by hand, and then colouring them in with whichever colour you chose. You could also pick your favourite design for a little pattern on the bracelet from a chart of about twenty.

While Andy and I were waiting for our bracelets at this stall, and the others were off buying other things, I asked Andy if Jacques had any explanation for the noises.

"I chickened out in the end," she replied. "I suddenly felt stupid talking about bumps in the night. I didn't want Jacques to think I was suggesting that it was him. It might sound like I was accusing him of something. The more I think about it, the more I think I must have imagined it."

"Let's see if the door is still locked at lunchtime when we get back," I suggested, and Andy seemed to think that this was a good idea. I glanced around me and suddenly spotted a bucket full of puppies, all cramped together, scrambling and falling over each other. "Look at those poor things," I said to Andy, then, as she was still waiting for her bracelet, I went over to take a closer look. I bent down and stroked them, and the man standing with them tried to interest me in buying one. He was gabbling away to me, but I couldn't understand a single word he was saying. I looked over to see if Andy was ready yet, then she could come and help me out, but she wasn't there. I straightened up and looked to the left and right of where she'd been standing, and there was no sign of her. Then, horror of horrors, I realized that someone was staring at me from near the book stall. It was Aline. I froze.

"*Salut*, Leah," she said, as she sauntered over to me with a horrible leer on her face.

"*Salut*," I replied, still looking round for Andy and praying that she'd show up quickly.

"*Ça va?*"

"*Oui, tres bien.*"

"*Et Andy, ta petite copine?*"

I didn't like her tone of voice, talking about my little friend Andy. "*Elle est ici*," I told her, so that she needn't think I was uncomfortable about being with her, because Andy was with me.

"*Tu restes chez Jacques?*"

I nodded and said "*Oui*," but I guessed she knew perfectly well that I was staying at Jacques's place. With every fibre in my body I wanted to get away from Aline, or to tell her that I hated her guts, but I've got no confidence when I'm on my own, so I just stood there, listening politely. Next she said something about Marie-Jo being very nice, and as best I could I told her that we would probably be going to Disneyland.

"Me too," she replied. "What a coincidence!" But I didn't like the way she said it, not one little bit.

It was then that I spotted Andy coming back, thank goodness. Aline noticed Andy coming at the same moment as I did, and quickly said "*Au revoir*," with a little wave of her hand and another of those leering grins, then she disappeared into the crowd. I couldn't see her anywhere by the time Andy was at my side.

"Were you talking to someone, Leah?"

"Aline."

"Aline! Where did she spring from?"

"She was standing staring at me with a really horrible expression on her face, and then she just started talking.

When I mentioned that we might be going to Disneyland, she said, 'Me too, what a coincidence!' with a really cunning look on her face that made me sick."

"Huh! She's just jealous. Anything you do she has to do too. Look, here come the others. Let's forget about that horrible girl and just enjoy ourselves, Leah, OK?" I nodded, because Andy made everything sound so normal and not worth bothering about, and I did try to forget about it after that, though I couldn't completely.

"Look, I went off to buy this ladybird for Sebastien. You know how he's obsessed with ladybirds at the moment? Well, look at this." She pulled out a soft-toy ladybird that was about five hundred times the size of a real one just in time for Jacques and the others to say how "*mignon*" and "*adorable*" it was.

We spent ages at the market and in the end Marie-Jo suggested we go to a special little place she knows for lunch. It was two o'clock, but apparently it didn't matter that we would be quite late. We drove about ten kilometres and stopped outside a very ordinary little place, which said "*Chez Katrine*" above the door. I don't know why, but I'd somehow imagined that we'd be going to a posh restaurant because the de Valloises were obviously well able to afford to eat in posh places. (How wonderful that must be!) When we went inside I couldn't believe it because, despite the fact that Jacques had tried to warn us that his mum was slightly weird in her taste for restaurants, this place was like a transport cafe.

"It's a *routier*," Andy whispered to me.

"What's that?"

"A transport cafe."

So I was right. We sat down at a formica-topped table, and I tried not to stare back at the lorry drivers in rough old clothes, who were staring at us. Then I noticed that one of them broke into a toothless grin and stood up.

"Marie-Jo!" he cried.

"Bertrand!" she shrieked delightedly, then she was in the midst of them all, kissing them and shaking their hands, exchanging bits of gossip and jokes, while we three looked on in amazement from our table, and Jacques looked at the menu as though he was used to this kind of scene.

Andy asked Jacques a few things, then translated for me. "Apparently Marie-Jo is loved by everyone who knows her, and she makes a point of being friendly with everyone from the chimney sweep to the high-court judge. Also, Jacques said that this might only be a *routier*, but the food is absolutely fantastic."

At that point Katrine appeared. She looked like a caricature, because she was very big on the top half and then, from the bottom of this enormous caftan-like shirt, emerged a pair of thin little legs. She greeted Marie-Jo as warmly as the lorry drivers had done and told her quickly what was for lunch, then drew close to her ear and whispered something. I had to wait for the translation until Jacques had whispered to Andy, who then turned to me.

"Apparently, Katrine always offers something extra-specially nice when Marie-Jo appears, even if she's got to start from scratch and make it then and there."

"I hope she doesn't start from scratch. I'm starving," I whispered back, just as Marie-Jo was saying to Katrine, "*Ah, non non non,*" followed by something that I gather

85

meant, "We'll stick to whatever's on today's menu."

Jacques was right. The food was delicious, and I loved the way we were all given plates, while the enormous dishes of meat and vegetables were left on the table for us to help ourselves – and then help ourselves to seconds, which we did! It was four-thirty by the time we got home, but we didn't care that it left hardly any time for the beach.

"We'll go and paddle in the sea at least," said Marie-Jo, smiling round at everyone, and I thought for the hundredth time how easy-going and thoughtful she was. "And how is my *cheri*?" she asked Serge, who came into the kitchen looking very tired.

"*Creve*," he answered, which apparently means "exhausted".

"Come and walk on the beach with us," Marie-Jo said, taking both his hands in hers and looking at him with her head tipped to one side. I was taking bets with myself on whether he'd be able to resist this idea. He couldn't, but I noticed that his face had turned serious, and he spoke softly to Marie-Jo.

When we all went off to get ready for the beach, Andy put her hand on my arm to hold me back. She waited till we were out of earshot of the others, then she said, "Did you hear what Serge said to Marie-Jo? That Lisa had come back and she was very tearful, but wouldn't say what was the matter."

Chapter 8

Tash

Celine and I are trying hard to get on well, but somehow, it isn't coming naturally to us. There's nothing majorly wrong, and I *am* having a good time – it's just that it's so difficult with the language barrier. We managed much better in England, and I realize now that that was because we were nearly always with loads of other people, English *and* French, whereas here, it looks as though I'm destined to spend the whole week away from Fen, at least. You see, after the revelation at the dinner table that the Lerois and the Leblancs don't get on very well (which probably means they hate each other's guts), I got Celine to tell me what had happened. She spoke in English and I helped her a lot. I sat there feeling absolutely appalled at the story. She finished with the words, "Maman and Papa don't forget, and the Leroi family will not forget. They want no more friendship with my family."

I lay in bed and tried to imagine what it would be like if something like that had happened between Fen's family and mine. What if Danny had babysat Rachel and Emmy three years ago and when he'd gone, Fen's dad had discovered that three videos and some money were missing. Then, when he'd questioned Danny about it, Danny had denied everything, and finally Mum had got angry with Fen's dad and said, "How *dare* you accuse my son of stealing your things." The more I thought about this, the more I felt sorry for Nicholas. I knew it was ridiculous of me to be taking sides when I'd only heard one half of the story, and I didn't know anything about it really, but I suppose it was because I knew I would have taken Danny's side. I had to admit I *was* rather prejudiced, though, and I knew Danny would *never* steal someone else's property. Anyway, it was pointless thinking about it, because Nicholas wasn't Danny. I rolled over and tried to go to sleep. Celine was already asleep.

After five minutes of staring at thin, wispy clouds floating across the grey-black sky through a fifteen-centimetre gap in the middle of the curtains, I realized that there was no chance of my going to sleep until I'd sorted out the problem between the Lerois and the Leblancs in my mind. I knew, obviously, that I couldn't solve it in real life, but I wanted to imagine what they *should* have done two years ago that would have improved their relationship since then.

In *my* version of events, had Danny been Nicholas, Mum would have got the truth from Danny, and if he *had* been guilty she would have marched him round to Fen's parents to apologize and give back the videos and money. But if he *hadn't* been guilty, she would have calmly told Fen's parents that she was sorry, but Danny was not responsible. What if Fen's parents hadn't believed her?

Then there would have been nothing that Mum could have done, but she wouldn't have stopped being friends with them. And I don't think they would have stopped being friends with Mum.

In the case of the Leblancs and the Lerois, it seemed to be both parties holding the grudge and refusing to be friends. That meant that Monsieur Leblanc must have been certain of his facts when he'd accused Nicholas, and Monsieur Leroi must have been equally positive that Nicholas couldn't have taken the videos and the money. But what about Nicholas himself? Had anyone really listened to what he had to say?

I was going round and round in circles and wished I could get the whole stupid thing out of my head. After all, it was nothing to do with me. Except that it had become something to do with me because it was stopping me and Fen from seeing each other. I could feel a frustrated anger building up inside me, and I decided that I was going to break the Tash mould and get to see Fen the following day even if I had to feign illness to achieve it. I was dying to see Nicholas, too. Maybe I'd try asking Madame Leblanc if I could phone, and if she said no again, I would pretend to be ill.

I was woken up by Celine excitedly reminding me that we had a great day ahead of us, and before I had time to remember my decision from the previous night, I jumped up, fresh as a daisy and said, "Oh yes, the monkey reserve and the picnic and the chateau and the forest!"

The moment I'd spoken I remembered that I had decided to pretend to be ill, and so far, I was displaying brilliant health. I'd have to eat an enormous breakfast then say I felt sick. What I really wanted to do was to talk to Fen, then I could find out what was happening at her end.

At breakfast time I asked Madame Leblanc if I could phone Fen, and she said it was a bit early. I asked if I could phone before we went out and she said that we'd be setting off fairly soon, so I'd better leave it till the evening. At that moment I felt really low because it would be impossible to pretend to be ill now. Madame Leblanc would know instantly that I was faking it. Also, she wouldn't just leave me on my own, would she? How stupid I'd been the previous night to imagine that such a ridiculous plan would work. Maybe it would be best just to tell Celine the truth and ask her to tell her mum that I was really missing the others and would it be all right to see them. I needn't specifically mention Fen. I was just considering this when the phone rang. Underneath the breakfast table I crossed my fingers. *Please let it be Fen.*

"Lucy," said Madame Leblanc with a smile, handing me the phone.

Great! "Hi, Luce. How are you?"

"It's not Luce. It's me," came Fen's whispering voice. "I didn't know if I'd be allowed to talk to you if I said it was me. Listen, I've got hardly any time at all because my money's about to run out."

"Your money? Where are you?"

"Public phone box. I said I was going out for a walk to take some photos. What are you doing today?"

I was about to tell her about the monkey reserve and the forest and everything, but Madame Leblanc was still around, wiping things, and I didn't really know how much she could understand. I decided the best bet would be to speak as fast as possible and use as many colloquial expressions as I could think of.

"Pretty action-packed day planned. What about you?"

"Something terrible's happened. Somebody spiked Sophie's and my drinks last night and we got drunk and behaved really badly. It wasn't our fault at all, but Madame Leroi is blaming me, because Sophie's never done anything like this before. She's not actually *said* that she's blaming me, but it's obvious that she is because she's acting so coldly towards me. I really badly want to see you and the others."

"Hasn't Sophie told her mum that it was someone else who spiked your drinks?"

"She's tried to, but her mum is just refusing to discuss it. She's trying to act normally, but I can tell she doesn't like me, and probably thinks I'm a really bad influence on Sophie."

"What are you going to do?"

"I'm going to get Sophie to tell her mum that we're both going into town, and I wondered if we could meet you there."

"Yeah. I'll persuade the powers-that-be round here to let us go off and meet the person that you're impersonating at the moment," I said, sticking to heavy code, "before we go out to the other places that were lined up."

"OK, in twenty minutes' time at the cafe nearest to the church in the centre of the village?"

"It may be better if I ask now. Hang on a sec." I turned to Madame Leblanc and spoke politely in slow English.

"Madame Leblanc, can Céline and I meet Lucy in the village, please, before we go out for the day?"

She saw that I was still on the phone and that she had, therefore, to make a decision quickly, which was exactly what I was relying on. "Yes, yes, of course."

"Thank you." I turned back to the phone. "That's fine, Luce. See you in twenty minutes."

At that very second the money must have run out, because I heard the "O" of "OK", then we were cut off. I said goodbye to the dead line, because I didn't want Madame Leblanc asking me any awkward questions about why Luce was on a public phone and not at Emma's.

So ten minutes later Céline and I were on our way down to the village. I had filled her in as best I could with my limited French on what had happened to Fen and Sophie. I'd had to look up the French word for drunk, and Sophie kept on gasping in disbelief all the way through my disjointed attempt at an account in French. We both wondered whether it was Nicholas who had spiked the drinks, and we were both dying to find out more from Fen.

As we went through the door to the café, it was lovely to see Fen and Sophie, all smiles at the sight of us two. Immediately all four started gabbling away at top speed, two of us in English, two of us in French. I glanced behind Fen's head at one point and noticed that just about everybody in the cafe was tuning in to us. They were all staring at us as though we'd left our space ship outside!

When we'd talked in twos for ages, and Céline and I had heard all about Nicholas's friend, Thibault, and the evening out that had ended so disastrously, the four of us began to talk together, which was a much slower process.

"There are two problems," began Fen, slowly, in English. The French girls nodded. "One: we've got to make sure your mum understands that Thibault put alcohol in our lemonades, and *that* made us act stupidly."

All three of us nodded. "It *was* Thibault, was it?" I asked, because I didn't know whether it had been the two boys playing a prank together, or just Thibault alone.

"Nicholas would never do something like that," Sophie defended her brother. We had settled into a pattern of all talking in our own languages, but very slowly.

"And the other problem is the one between your two families. It can't go on," Fen continued.

"We agree, but how can any of us stop it? These are adults who refuse to meet and talk," said Sophie.

"So we make them meet and talk," said Fen.

"What can they say?" asked Sophie. "Celine's father will say, 'Nicholas stole videos and money,' and my father will say, 'No, he did not.' That will be the end of the talking."

"And what would Nicholas say, I wonder?" I asked.

"He said no before, so he will say no again."

"I think they have been long enough without talking," I couldn't help saying.

Celine hadn't said anything so far, but she was looking very thoughtful indeed.

"I think Tash is right," she said, her eyes gleaming at the rest of us. "I think we should have the meeting today. This is the plan."

So we all huddled closer at the table, our elbows practically touching, while Celine slowly and carefully told us

93

her plan. Thirty-five minutes later, we had paid for our drinks and walked home, us to Celine's, the other two to Sophie's, and twenty minutes after that we were on our way to the monkey reserve at Touraneuf. Monsieur Leblanc, Katrine and Victoria were with us, too. I felt very honoured! The rest of the morning was great. We wandered round acres and acres of forest, where all sorts of different species of monkeys lived in families. They really acted like proper families, with each member of the family having responsibilities. The nicest sight was of monkeys grooming each other.

"It reminds me of when Fen and I both had head lice at primary school," I said to Celine, but I didn't know the French for lice, so I said insects of the head, and she told me that the word was "*les poux*". Then we had a laugh when I explained to her what the English word "poo" meant!

We were allowed to feed the monkeys, but were told to do it carefully, not because there was any danger, but so as not to frighten them and make them react badly to future visitors to the reserve. Celine and I were constantly looking around to see whether Fen's scheme was beginning to work. You see, if all had gone according to plan, Fen, Sophie, and the rest of the Leroi family should also be in the monkey reserve.

At exactly one-thirty we planned to "accidentally on purpose" come across them in the picnic area. Apparently the Leroi family had been to the reserve quite a few times before and had had lunch in the cafe. The last time they'd been, Monsieur Leroi had commented that he didn't think much of the cafe, but he thought the picnic area looked lovely, and that the next time they came, they should bring a picnic. As the Leblancs had already planned spending the morning at the monkey reserve, it seemed the perfect solution for the great reunion to take place there. I felt very nervous. I was worried that they might well take one look at Celine's family and walk away in disgust. I could tell Celine was nervous too, because she kept biting her lip. On the other hand, they might not actually turn up at all, in which case I would feel really sorry for Fen, and very disappointed that our great plan had been thwarted.

By one-twenty-five, Celine and I were nervous wrecks. We knew we had to act very quickly indeed the moment we caught sight of the Lerois, and Fen and Sophie had to act quickly too, because the idea was that Celine and I would each grab the hand of either Victoria or Katrine and rush over to Sophie and Fen, then after a two-second "Hi, how are you?" we'd go over to Monsieur and Madame Leroi and Celine would introduce me to them as innocently as anything. At the same time, Sophie would be introducing Fen to Celine's parents. We had realized that during this, the two fathers might simply walk away, finding it all too embarrassing to cope with, but that wasn't too serious, because all we had to do was to hang on to the mothers and gradually bring them together. The reason we wanted to keep Katrine and Victoria at our sides was because there was less chance of Celine's parents walking away if the little girls weren't with them. And if the fathers *did* go off, they'd only get as far as their cars, because they could hardly drive off without their families.

We hadn't really got much further with our masterplan

than this. I think we all kind of hoped that by some wonderful miracle, everybody would get talking and agree to let bygones be bygones, and they'd all live happily ever after. The other possibility, of course, was that nothing at all would happen, that the two families would be polite but distant, say the minimum to each other, then go their separate ways and carry on exactly as before. And there *was* a fourth possibility, only I didn't like to think about this one. Madame Leroi and Madame Leblanc might realize instantly that we four had cooked up the whole thing, and they might be furious and ground us for the rest of the week.

"Nearly half past one," I whispered to Celine. "Say something."

"I'm starving, Maman. Can we have the picnic now?"

"Me too," said Monsieur Leblanc. "Let's go and sit down."

"Look, it says 'Picnic area' on that sign," continued Celine.

Madame Leblanc looked pleased that we'd found somewhere to eat so quickly, and off we went.

By this time, I knew there was no chance of a single morsel of food passing my lips, and the inside of my mouth felt really dry. I was searching the whole place for Fen and the Lerois, but the nearer we got the more convinced I was that they weren't there. We sat down at a large table with benches attached, and Celine and I made sure we'd chosen a table on the edge of the picnic area, and that we were facing the rest of the tables, whereas Celine's parents had their backs to them. Victoria sat on our side of the table, and Katrine on her parents' side.

Celine and I picked at our food and kept up our constant surveillance of the area.

"You two are very curious," said Monsieur Leblanc in English. I tried my best not to blush.

"I'm always like this. Mum tells me to stop staring every time we're at a cafe or anywhere like that," I gabbled in English.

"*En français, en français*," laughed Madame Leblanc. "*Je ne comprends pas!*"

So I tried my best, with everybody's help, to repeat it in French. At least it lightened the atmosphere a bit, and I relaxed for a moment because I was off my guard. That, of course, was the very moment that Fen and Sophie suddenly appeared with Madame Leroi. Madame Leroi was chatting away in the middle of them, but Fen and Sophie were looking frantically round. There was no sign of Monsieur Leroi or his son. Right! Action!

"Sophie!" yelled Celine, with beautifully faked surprise.

"Fen!" I followed suit. "Come and see Fen," I said to Victoria, yanking her off the bench, while Celine, who'd forgotten about Katrine and was halfway across to Sophie, came dashing back for Katrine, then hared off again. I couldn't help catching the look of mild bewilderment on the faces of Celine's parents, because, of course, they hadn't clicked that they were about to be thrust into the company of the enemy.

"*Bonjour*, Madame Leroi," I said, kissing her quickly in true French fashion.

She looked rather taken aback, but nevertheless quite pleased, I thought, and she asked me how I was getting on. I said "*Chouette, merci*," which made her laugh – I must have pronounced it wrongly or something – but I was glad I was amusing her. I asked her where Monsieur Leroi was, but she didn't need to answer because round the corner came a boy who looked very much like Danny, actually, with a man who was presumably Monsieur Leroi. The man frowned when he saw that Celine was standing next to his wife, and stopped in his tracks for a moment, but Nicholas kept walking, so his father had to, too. I went leaping over to him, showing massive confidence that I didn't feel at all, and stuck out my hand. "*Bonjour, Monsieur. Je suis Tash, la correspondante de Celine.*" I smiled a big smile, and then I turned to Nicholas, who looked quite different from Danny close up. In fact he looked really nice. He was already looking at me, and when he broke into a smile, I suddenly understood what people mean when they talk about their hearts melting.

Chapter 9

Andy

It had shocked me on that first night to find that Lisa's bedroom door was locked. I'd gone through all kinds of explanations for this in my head. Then, in the morning, I'd told Leah what I'd done and she obviously thought I was out of my mind, creeping about in the middle of the night. I was curious to see whether Lisa would show up at breakfast, but she didn't.

Jacques's mum is probably the nicest woman I know, apart from Mum, of course. We had a great time at the market and stayed there for far longer than we'd expected, and then Marie-Jo had insisted on taking us to this little transport cafe that she loves. We could tell why it was such a favourite with her. There was a brilliant atmosphere in there and the food was lovely, and masses of it. All these rough-looking lorry drivers turned into charming gentlemen when they saw Marie-Jo. They all knew her and were obviously delighted to see her. That's another quality of Marie-Jo's, the fact that she gets on with everyone, no matter whether she has anything in common with them or not.

There was still just about time to go to the beach when we'd finished our incredibly late lunch, but we had to go home first. It was when we were there that Serge, who had been working at home all morning, whispered to Marie-Jo that Lisa had returned and was upset about something.

"Where is the poor child? In her room? Let me go and see her," Marie-Jo immediately said, looking very concerned, and again I thought how nice and tolerant she was.

"She doesn't seem to want to go into her room. She's in the conservatory," Serge told his wife, so off went Marie-Jo to find Lisa, while we went to our rooms to get ready for the beach. When we came down five minutes later, Marie-Jo was back in the kitchen wearing a frown and sitting quite still at the kitchen table.

"What's the matter, Maman?" asked Jacques.

"Lisa won't talk to me. I can't understand it."

"She may talk to Andy and Leah," suggested Jacques. "Maybe it's just that she can't manage to say what she wants to say in French."

"Good thinking, Jacques," said Marie-Jo, brightening up immediately. "Come on, Leah and Andy. Let me introduce you to Lisa."

She was sitting curled up in a white wicker chair by some beautiful white flowers that I think were lilacs. She had long fair hair and was quite pretty. She looked more worried than ever when she saw two strangers trailing behind Marie-Jo, and she also looked a bit weepy as though she'd been crying just before.

"Lisa, *ma chere*," began Marie-Jo. "We have Andy and

Leah staying here with us, and they are both English. This is Andy, who is also half French, and this is Leah."

"Hello," Leah and I said in unison. I don't know about her but I felt pretty silly, because I hadn't a clue what to say next. I could hardly say, "So why are you crying? Come on, you can tell me, because I'm English." For a start, Lisa was eighteen. She wouldn't want to confide in a little thirteen-year-old. Somebody had to say something, though, because Marie-Jo had very unsubtly left the conservatory, taking Jacques and Laurette with her.

"I thought you were back because I heard a noise from your room last night. Yours is the room above ours, I think," I began.

Her eyes turned on me as though I'd announced that I was thirty-two years of age and a fully qualified teenage psychologist, so she could just spit out her problems and I would sort everything out for her.

"You heard a noise?" she said slowly. "What kind of noise?"

"Er, a bang. At least it sounded like a bang from below. I mean, as though someone had dropped something."

Her expression had changed slightly. She was looking more worried than shocked now.

"Oh, not that it disturbed me or anything," I quickly reassured her. "I just assumed you were back and that you'd dropped something."

"But I wasn't, and I didn't," she said slowly. "I only came back today."

"Well, I must have been mistaken then," I said, thinking that so far the conversation wasn't going very well at all.

I could have told Marie-Jo it would be hopeless giving me the job of sympathetic, understanding listener. I'm just not the type. I was on the point of handing over to Leah and going off to find the others when Lisa started to talk and talk.

"No, you weren't mistaken, and I'm so pleased I'm not the only one to have heard the noise. It's been driving me mad. Not every night, of course, but maybe every third night. In the end I just had to get away. I couldn't tell Marie-Jo about it, because of her beliefs. Then I decided I *had* to come back because I love the job and I love Bastien and I knew he'd be missing me. I thought I'd try and tell Serge, and just pray that he didn't have the same beliefs as Marie-Jo. So I tried to tell him, but I didn't know the word for poltergeist, and then when he was acting so kindly towards me, even though I'd just walked out without a word of explanation, I suddenly broke down in tears, and couldn't recover. I didn't know what to do. Thank goodness *you're* not being nice to me, otherwise I'd burst into tears again. Oh, I didn't mean that you're being horrible or anything, I just meant that you weren't putting your arm round me and asking me what's the matter. You're just talking normally."

"Actually, I've hardly said anything at all," I quickly put in, because I was afraid that Lisa would never stop if someone didn't stop her.

"And I haven't said *anything*," Leah added, with a smile.

Lisa seemed to look at us properly then. "Sorry, I *do* go on, don't I, but I'm just so pleased to find that I'm not the only one hearing bumps in the night."

"Actually, I went upstairs to investigate," I confessed.

"And?" asked Lisa, uncurling herself from the chair and leaning forwards.

"And the door was locked," I replied.

"Locked? I wonder who's locked my door? It wasn't me!"

"I don't know."

"What did you mean when you mentioned Marie-Jo's beliefs?" asked Leah.

"Well, the only time that Marie-Jo has ever got cross with me was when she found me reading this particular book to Bastien about six months ago. Bastien's learning English at school, and Marie-Jo is keen for me to try and encourage him to speak a bit of English with me, so last time I went back to England, I came back with a selection of stories. I deliberately chose books that were too young for Bastien because I knew the text would be easier.

"Anyway, the story I was reading to him when she came in was all about a ghost, and she looked over my shoulder and listened for a minute or two, then she suddenly went spare, and said there were no such things as ghosts and on no account was I to fill Bastien's head with such rubbish. I was gobsmacked, I can tell you, because Marie-Jo is never cross with anyone, and it was just as though she'd completely flipped. I didn't know what to think and I was expecting her to have another go at me later, but the next time I saw her she was her normal smiling self and it was just as though the whole episode had never happened. She's never said anything since, and neither has Bastien.

"When I first heard a noise in my bedroom about a

week ago I didn't think too much about it. I don't scare easily, and I just figured it was one of those unexplained noises in the night, but nothing to worry about. The problem was when I heard exactly the same noise the following night, but even then I managed to keep my cool, and I just told myself it was the hot-water cistern filling up or something like that. But two nights later when exactly the same noise came again, I was lying waiting for it, and wondering if and when it would come, because I'd had one night without any noise at all. My senses must have been totally heightened and the noise sounded just as though it was beside the bed. I immediately snapped the night light on and took a look round the room but nothing appeared to be different. Then I noticed one of my slippers in the very place where I'd heard the noise, and I was certain I'd left both my slippers together, and that's when I started to think there might be a poltergeist in the room.

"I knew it was stupid of me, because this house is modern and I didn't think poltergeists haunted modern places. Then I did some reading about them and realized that actually they're just noisy spirits, so they could come from anywhere, and choose where they want to carry out their furniture moving – or in my case slipper moving. And let's face it, if *you* were a poltergeist, and you had a choice of where to live, wouldn't you choose a palace like this, rather than a little end-of-terrace house? I know I would."

The more Lisa talked, the more I liked her. She wasn't anything at all like me in character. She was probably most like Luce. She had a really vivid imagination and she was very emotional and talked a lot, just like Luce. I sneaked a sideways glance at Leah and she gave me the trace of a look that said that she definitely agreed with me. All the same I felt sorry for Lisa, because she had obviously been scared. I wanted to know what had finally driven her away.

"There were two more nights without a sound, though I hardly slept at all, because I lay there petrified, just waiting for the noise. After the second night I decided that the poltergeist probably didn't want to appear when I'd got the night light on, and I knew the answer was simply to leave the light on every night, then I'd never have to hear any noises again. The trouble was that I couldn't sleep with the light on. Never have been able to, and never will, so I gave myself a big talking-to and told myself that there was nothing to fear. I knew that the noise wasn't a burglar or anything like that, so I would just have to accept that if a poltergeist wanted to move my slipper or anything else, then fine. It didn't worry me. It wasn't harming me, was it? Then I closed my eyes and felt myself drifting off to sleep.

"Well, you can imagine my shock when that very same noise, right beside the bed, jolted me awake. It was all I could do not to scream the place down. I lay there with my heart beating like a big bass drum. After all my 'it-doesn't-worry-me' talk, I was a wreck. I put the light on, though half of me wanted just to hide under the bed-clothes. I took a good look round and there was nothing to be seen. What's more, I'd memorized where everything was in the room before I'd gone to sleep, and absolutely nothing was in the wrong place. Well, that did it. I hardly slept a wink all night, and I knew I wouldn't be able to spend another night in the place, but I didn't dare tell anyone. I thought that if Marie-Jo got to hear about my strange fancies she'd either flip again, or otherwise she'd consider me unfit to look after her son and she'd get rid of me. I decided I'd pretend I had a crisis in my life and I was going off to sort it out. I know I shocked Marie-Jo when I told her I was going away for a few days, but she never told me off or anything, just said I must tell her if there was any way in which she could help. It was such a ridiculous situation, because if it had been any other problem but poltergeists, she would have been the best person in the world to help me, because she's so nice and warm. But I'll never forget the way she flipped over that ghost story."

Lisa had been talking non-stop for ages. I thought she must be exhausted. It was certainly an incredible story, and I wasn't sure what to say now she'd finished. It was Leah who spoke, and I was glad.

"I think you've got to tell Marie-Jo," she said slowly and sympathetically. "It's the only option you've got, really. You needn't even mention the word 'poltergeist'. Just say that you were terrified by noises in the night, and you took off because you hadn't slept for two nights and you were in such a state that you couldn't think properly."

Lisa seemed to be considering this idea. The trouble was, she didn't have any time to consider it, because at that very moment in walked Marie-Jo. She looked very concerned.

"Would anyone like a drink before we go to the beach?"

We all shook our heads and I nodded at Lisa to tell her

to say something, but her lips tightened a tiny bit as though she'd made the decision that she couldn't speak.

"Would you like to join us, Lisa? We're all off to the beach."

"Lisa's got something to tell you," I said impulsively before I could change my mind.

Immediately Lisa's expression changed to one of horror, but Marie-Jo was sitting in the wicker chair opposite her and looking sympathetic. For at least a minute there was silence. Leah and I flashed each other looks, but neither of us wanted to interfere. After another few seconds, though, I couldn't bear it any longer.

"Lisa thought she heard a noise in the night," I began in French, then I looked at Lisa to see if she could continue from that start. She must have been completely tongue-tied, because she didn't utter a word. Or maybe she was just exhausted after having told the whole thing to Leah and me.

"A noise? What kind of noise?" asked Marie-Jo.

"A bang," I told her, after a few seconds had elapsed and I was sure that Lisa was still unable to speak. "She'd heard the same noise quite a few times and it was driving her mad because there didn't seem to be a reason for it."

Lisa nodded. I could tell she had managed to follow what I was saying in French.

"Oh, my poor girl," said Marie-Jo, frowning at Lisa sympathetically, then looking up, as though the bang might suddenly put in an appearance from the ceiling, and explain itself. "I am trying to think what this noise could be," Marie-Jo went on. "Did it seem to come from above you or below you, Lisa?"

Again, Lisa had no problem understanding. I realized

that her French was pretty good. She answered in French. "It was like a thud on the floor beside my bed. And Andy heard it too, didn't you, Andy?"

"Yes, I heard a noise like something being dropped on to the ceiling above me last night. The other two were asleep." I was debating whether or not to tell Marie-Jo that I'd then gone upstairs to investigate. I decided not to. "I think Lisa's room is directly above ours, isn't it?" She nodded. "I just thought that she must have come back after all."

"You see, that proves that there is something in the room," said Lisa, getting excited all of a sudden.

"Something? What do you mean?" asked Marie-Jo. Lisa must have realized her mistake the moment she'd spoken, because she was suggesting the very thing that she knew would make Marie-Jo cross.

"I don't mean anything. I just mean that I couldn't have been imagining it if Andy heard it too."

"Yes, bizarre!" murmured Marie-Jo. "Let's go and look up there. May we go into your room, Lisa?"

"Yes, of course. I'm not hiding anything."

"I didn't think for a moment that you were," smiled Marie-Jo. "I'll get the key from the kitchen and we'll have a look together. We'll play detectives."

"You locked my room?" asked Lisa.

"Yes, of course. I wanted you to be sure that your property is quite safe in our house, so I locked it for you until you came back."

"Thank you," mumbled Lisa, sounding at a loss for what to say. Marie-Jo must have been the most thoughtful person under the sun.

Jacques and Laurette were in the kitchen, looking bored. They both jumped to their feet when they saw us come in.

"Are we ready to go now?" asked Jacques.

"In a moment," answered his mother.

"What's happening?" whispered Laurette to me, getting up and following us out of the kitchen. I hung back a bit with Laurette as our little party made its way up to Lisa's room, which was quite a trek in such a big house. As we walked along I explained in whispers to Laurette what Lisa had told us. I kept it fairly brief and to the point. When I said, "Lisa thought it was a poltergeist," Laurette shot me a shocked look and said, "A poltergeist?" Marie-Jo suddenly swung round and faced Laurette and me, then Lisa. It was obvious that she'd heard Laurette. Laurette mouthed, "Sorry", to me. There was nothing I could do.

"You thought it was a poltergeist, Lisa?"

"That was all I could think," Lisa said.

"And is that why you felt you couldn't tell me about it?" Lisa nodded.

"Oh, my poor girl," said Marie-Jo, for the second time that afternoon, as she approached Lisa and put her arm round her. "I am a terrible person. You thought I would be cross, didn't you?" Again Lisa nodded. "Because I was cross about the ghost story you were reading to Bastien?" Another nod from Lisa, while the rest of us watched and listened in wide-eyed interest. "I'm such a scatterbrain. I completely forgot about that silly outburst of mine until just now. The thing is, I wasn't really cross with you, although I know it must have seemed to you that I was. You see, Bastien had been terrified of ghosts until just before you came to live with us, Lisa. Night after night he had had nightmares about ghosts. We never knew why. But then shortly after you came, the nightmares stopped. Just like that! Bastien seemed completely cured. So when I heard you reading the story it brought it all back so vividly that I think I just flipped. I suddenly had a flash-back to all those terrible sleepless nights that we'd all suffered, and I felt as though I could almost hear the sound of Bastien's screams in my ears."

"I thought you had strong religious beliefs, or some-thing. And then when you never mentioned it again, I thought it was because you couldn't bear even to talk about the subject, so when these noises started, I wondered if you knew there was a ghost in the house. It drove me round the bend."

Lisa had been talking in French, but she said this last sentence in English and Marie-Jo broke into a smile and repeated it slowly, as though enjoying the phrase.

"It drove me round the bend." Her expression turned serious again almost immediately. "You poor child."

"I'm eighteen."

"You're a child to me, and I feel terrible for having made you suffer so. Let's go and sort this ghost out. There must be some explanation. And if we don't find one, you can choose another room."

When Marie-Jo unlocked the door and turned the handle slowly, we all stood still as statues.

"*Bonjour, Monsieur le fantome*," she said, with a grin at us all as she flung the door open. And to everyone's sur-prise, out rushed a grey mottled cat. "Mimi! So that's where you've been hiding, is it?"

"But how did she get in?" Lisa asked.

"Through the window," replied Marie-Jo.

"But the window's shut!" said Leah.

"But when I was here the window was open," Lisa said thoughtfully as Laurette and I hurried over to it. Laurette opened it and leant out.

"She climbed up the ivy," she said, "and in through the window."

"Then she plopped on to the floor, with a thud," I added, raising my eyebrows at Lisa.

Lisa and Marie-Jo both shot a look at me, then slowly faced each other. When they spoke it was in unison.

"So Mimi is the ghost!"

Chapter 10

Fen

When I woke up the morning after the fateful evening, I didn't know where I was at first. All I knew was that I had a steel band around my skull. At least, that's what it felt like. Slowly the memory of that awful evening came back, though I couldn't remember things clearly. I could remember the cinema, of course, and going to the cafe afterwards, and Thibault getting the drinks, and my lemonade tasting very bitter. That was it! Thibault spiked our drinks. He must have asked the barman to put something alcoholic in our lemonades. I don't know how we didn't realize at the time. I felt so stupid.

I don't know how we made it home, either. I can remember walking into a tree at one point, and I can remember Celine giggling uncontrollably. I've got some vague memory of some CDs breaking, and of me trying to pour something back into a bottle. Then the next thing I knew, Monsieur and Madame Leroi were standing there looking as though Celine and I had done something awful, but all we'd done was. . .

We'd got drunk, we'd smashed some of their CDs, we'd

helped ourselves to their alcohol. We'd spilt it everywhere, and to complete the list of crimes, we didn't appear to care about any of this. So that's the effect that alcohol can have on you. You don't know what you're doing. You have no control over what you say or what you do. Suddenly I wanted to kill Thibault. He made me sick. How dare he take such liberties with two thirteen-year-old girls? And what did he do it for, anyway? What did he gain from it, apart from a cheap laugh? I couldn't understand why Nicholas was friends with him because Nicholas seemed really nice, but Thibault was a nasty piece of work.

I raised my head from the pillow but dropped it straight back down again because it throbbed. Then a big depression set in, because I bet I knew how Madame Leroi would punish Sophie and me. She'd ground us. Or if she didn't ground us completely, she'd definitely prevent us from seeing Tash, and maybe from seeing all the others as well. I couldn't bear it. I had to do something. The first thing was to wake Sophie.

Waking Sophie proved easier said than done. She just groaned and turned away from me, then when I persisted, she buried herself further and further down under her duvet. In the end I had to take the whole duvet away from her. That made her open her eyes and sit bolt upright, but she must have had the same headache that I had, because she flopped back down again and lay quite still, staring up at the ceiling. I threw the duvet back over her then and decided to leave her for a minute or two, because I knew what she was doing. She was slowly piecing together the events of the previous evening, just like I had done a few minutes before. When she heaved a big sigh and closed her eyes, I spoke.

"Sophie, what are we going to do?"

"Apologize and beg."

I'm not sure that I translated literally what Sophie said in French, but I think that was the general gist of it.

"And explain," I added.

"*Oui, expliquer*," she agreed.

So we got washed and dressed slowly, then went downstairs to face the lion in its den. Personally I was dreading seeing Sophie's parents. It was going to be just too embarrassing for words. Monsieur Leroi was nowhere to be seen, thank goodness, but Madame was in the kitchen being very brisk and businesslike. She said, "*Bonjour, les filles*," when we appeared, and asked if we'd slept well, and started slamming dishes and spoons and things down on the kitchen table, but I could tell that despite her attempts at the occasional smile, she was seething underneath.

I nudged Sophie and she began the apologetic, begging, explaining speech. I couldn't understand it all, but it sounded like she was making a very thorough job of it. Every so often I said "*Oui*" to show that the speech was also on my behalf. I was watching Madame Leroi like a hawk to see what her reaction was. I got the impression, from the way she gradually slowed down her dish-flinging activities, and sat with her chin cupped in her hands and her elbows on the table, that she was prepared to listen, but that she wasn't quite ready to forgive us.

At one point, when I heard Sophie say the words "Thibault" and "*alcohol*" I did a vigorous nod, which made Madame Leroi flash a quick look at me before her eyes went back to Sophie. I had the horrible feeling that Madame Leroi wasn't convinced that the culprit was Thibault, because, after all, she'd known him for years, and it was a much better bet that the visitor from England was to blame. My face went pale and my heart lurched when I had this thought, because I could easily see why Madame Leroi's mind should work in this way. I mean, she didn't really know anything about me, did she? Maybe I was always getting drunk at home, and helping myself to other people's alcohol, and smashing up their CDs. The worst thing of all was that when Monsieur and Madame Leroi had appeared in the sitting room, it was to find Yours Truly pouring the alcohol back into the bottle, just as though I'd heard them coming, and tried to hide the evidence.

When Sophie came to the end of her apology, Madame Leroi said, "*Hm. Nous verrons bien.*" Then she encouraged us to eat breakfast, and she acted coolly but not coldly towards us. It was just as though she hadn't made up her mind about the situation yet. When Madame Leroi was out of the room for a minute, I asked Sophie what "*Nous verrons bien*" meant, and she said it meant, "We will see."

After breakfast, Madame Leroi told us that she was going out for a short time with Monsieur Leroi, and that when they returned we would consider the rest of the day. I asked if I could nip out to post some postcards and she said that was fine. Sophie didn't want to come with me. I took a ten-franc piece and rushed off to the nearest phone box. I could remember passing one on the way to the cinema.

It was lovely to talk to Tash and even better to know that I was going to see her in a few minutes, because that's what we arranged. Sophie was delighted when I rushed back to the house and told her what I'd done, so the two of us told Madame Leroi that we were going for a walk into the village, and off we went to meet Tash and Celine.

Tash and I have never talked faster in our lives. We had so much to catch up on. Then the four of us discussed how we could possibly get the two families to stop their ridiculous feud. Celine had a plan to try and get them back together again as friends, but there were absolutely no guarantees that her scheme would even begin to work. When she'd explained it all, we split up and went our separate ways, all crossing our fingers that we'd meet up later.

The first obstacle to overcome was the fact that Sophie's mum didn't want to take us out till later, and for the plan to work we needed to go out as soon as possible. We'd picked the monkey reserve as the best place for the two families to meet because it wasn't far away, and because Sophie said her family had been there several times and had always enjoyed it.

When we got back from meeting the others we flew into the house so that Sophie could beg her mother to take us to the monkey reserve. We also needed to be sure that Monsieur Leroi and Nicholas could come, too. I was beginning to think that we'd been relying on too many things working out exactly as we wanted them to.

"Where's Maman?" Sophie asked Nicholas, who was drinking coffee at the kitchen table when we went in. I noticed he was giving us searching looks, as if trying to suss out how we felt. I was glad that we didn't appear to be suffering, because I wasn't entirely sure whether Nicholas was in on the big joke with Thibault, or whether the whole drink-spiking thing had been Thibault's doing.

"She's gone out," Nicholas replied briefly, before lowering his head again. He definitely was not in the mood for communicating.

"How are you?" he then asked me.

"Better," I replied, my eyes boring into his, to show him I did not appreciate his sense of humour, if he had been responsible.

"It was Thibault, not me," he said, putting his hands up as if in surrender. "He told me what he had done when you left the cafe."

I had to ask Nicholas to repeat that last bit because I couldn't translate it straight away.

"You had no idea until after?" I asked slowly in English.

"No idea, I promise," he replied. He'd almost snapped the answer at me and I noticed he was looking very black and thundery. I wasn't sure if he was cross with Thibault or not, but I definitely believed him when he said he'd had no idea what Thibault had been up to.

"Where has Maman gone?" Sophie tried again.

"She would not say," Nicholas answered, but again his reply was very abrupt. Something was definitely eating away at him. "I told her it was Thibault, and she said she was going out with Papa," he added.

"Do you think they've gone to Thibault's?" I asked, as best I could.

"No. I told them not to. I don't know where they've gone."

"We want to go to the monkey reserve when they get back," Sophie went on. "Will you come too, Nicholas?"

"I – "

"Please," I said in a begging voice. And that clinched it, because I suppose Nicholas was still feeling that he had to make up in some way for Thibault's behaviour.

"OK."

"When will your parents be back?" I asked.

Nicholas just shrugged to show he'd no idea. His eyes stared into his coffee cup, and Sophie jerked her head at the door, as if to say, "There's no point in talking to Nicholas when he's like this." So out we went.

"Why don't we give your mum a lovely surprise and tidy up the whole house?" I suggested in slow French to Sophie.

At first she thought I'd completely lost my marbles, because she said her head hurt too much, and she wasn't used to doing housework, but it didn't take me long to convince her that this would be the best thing we could possibly do if we were to have any chance at all of getting to that monkey reserve. So we set to work.

An hour later, my head felt much better, and Sophie and I were putting the finishing touches to the sitting room, having made the rest of the house spotless. I had enjoyed doing this work because I like surprising people and I quite like having big clear-up sessions, anyway. I'd realized during the past hour that Sophie wasn't kidding when she'd said that she wasn't used to housework. She worked much more slowly than I did, and she shook her head in amazement at the sight of me polishing the table top vigorously, and loading the dishwasher in seconds. The sitting room was almost ready. I just had to whiz the vacuum round, while Sophie plumped up the cushions.

The noise of the vacuum cleaner stopped us from noticing that the sitting-room door had opened, and when I looked up I got a shock to see Monsieur and Madame Leroi standing there. I quickly switched off the vacuum cleaner and more or less stood to attention, feeling for a second as though *I* was part of the house inspection, too. Sophie stood beside me and we waited. Madame Leroi looked from us to the mantelpiece with the ornaments all spaced out neatly, to the television and the two perfect piles of videos beside it, and then slowly her eyes took in the rest of the room. Monsieur Leroi took a moment longer to realize what had been happening in his absence. He was still staring at the gleaming polished sideboard, but Madame Leroi had whizzed off to the kitchen, flung the door open and returned in seconds.

"*Incroyable!*" she exclaimed, breaking into a smile. Then she turned to her husband and explained that the kitchen was "*transformee*" as well.

"We've done the whole house," beamed Sophie at her parents. "Fen did much more than me, though."

I thought I had understood that bit correctly, and a moment later I was sure, because Madame Leroi came over to me and said, "What an adorable girl" (to translate literally), as she put her arm round me and gave me a big kiss.

"What about me? Aren't I adorable?" asked Sophie, looking very crestfallen. That made both her parents laugh

119

heartily and Monsieur Leroi assured Sophie she was adorable too, then turned to me and spoke in English.

"We are sorry that you have had a bad start to your
holiday with us, because of the friend of our son, but now
we hope all will be well again. Where shall we go out to
this morning? Is there anywhere special you wish to visit?"

My eyes met Sophie's. "I'd love to see the monkey
reserve," I replied happily. "Sophie has told me all about
it."

Less than an hour later we were there. Sophie and I
had continued in our "busy bee" mode, and made the
fastest picnic known to man. Then we'd all piled into the
car.

So far so good, I said to myself. Things couldn't really
have been any better because the whole Leroi family
seemed to be in an excellent mood. We had only been
told that the parents had gone for a walk together, presumably to talk about what had happened the previous
evening. It wasn't until we were in the monkey reserve,
and Sophie had gone on ahead with her mother, but I
had hung back a bit, that I realized exactly what Monsieur
and Madame Leroi had been discussing on their walk.
You see, Nicholas and his dad hadn't realized that I had
hung back to feed one of the monkeys. I was crouching
down, close to this beautiful baby monkey who was nib-
bling nuts from my hand, when the two of them strolled
past me, deep in conversation, without noticing me.
Naturally they were talking in French, but it didn't take
the best linguist in the world to work out that Monsieur
Leroi wanted to tell Thibault off, but Nicholas was trying
to persuade him just to let things rest. I gathered that

Thibault had made Nicholas's life a misery for quite some time, and Monsieur Leroi was telling Nicholas that he didn't have to put up with it, and that he must stand up to Thibault.

They stopped talking and watched a pair of monkeys chasing each other up and down the branches of two trees, soaring through the air from one outstretched branch to the other with the greatest of ease. It was an incredible display of agility, and I stood beside Nicholas for a minute before running on to catch up with the others. Until I saw the anxious expression on Sophie's face, I had no idea that we were fast approaching the picnic area. She beckoned to me to catch up when her mother wasn't looking, and we whispered together briefly before bracing ourselves and entering the area. As we entered, Madame Leroi was chatting away to us both, but we were scanning the place.

Immediately I spotted Tash and Celine sitting at one of those tables with benches attached, facing us with one of the little sisters, while her parents and the other little sister had their backs to us.

"Sophie!" cried Celine, jumping up and belting over to us.

"Fen!" cried Tash, in a perfect imitation, as though she was taking the mickey. Tash grabbed one of the little girls and rushed over to us, kissing Madame Leroi, and Celine went back for the other little sister, who she'd forgotten. This was all exactly as we'd planned it. But where were Nicholas and Monsieur Leroi? I'd thought they were only just behind. At that point Madame Leroi broke into happy laughter at something that Tash had said and Madame Leblanc turned round and saw Madame Leroi. The two women managed to exchange something that passed as a smile, then Nicholas and his father appeared.

"*Bonjour, Monsieur. Je suis Tash, la correspondante de Celine*," said Tash.

Tash looked over at Nicholas, and something came over her face. I'd never seen that expression on Tash's face before, and when I looked at Nicholas I thought he looked exactly the same. I was shocked, because this bit definitely hadn't been in the script! The look that was passing between them was so strong that for a moment the awfulness of the two families being within twenty metres of each other was forgotten.

I quickly introduced Tash and Nicholas and that broke the spell. They both suddenly looked very confused, then Nicholas kissed Tash on the cheek. Monsieur and Madame Leroi both shook hands with her, and I rushed after Sophie, who had remembered what we had planned and was greeting Monsieur and Madame Leblanc. The two men called out a rather sharp "*Bonjour*" across the picnic area, and then Monsieur and Madame Leroi sat down at a table that was just about as far away from the Leblancs as it was possible to be. Quite a few of the tables were occupied, but there was a free one much closer to the Leblancs.

Celine went back to her own family and invited Sophie and me to stay at their table with them. The Leblancs didn't seem to mind at all. At this point Tash was supposed to be here too, so that there wouldn't be enough room left for Monsieur and Madame Leblanc at their table, and Sophie was supposed to deliver the punch line: "Maman, there's no room for Celine's parents here. Can they sit with you?"

The trouble was, there *was* room, because Tash and Victoria were still standing with Nicholas, Tash looking totally star-struck. She suddenly came back to earth and realized that she was supposed to be back at the Leblancs' table, but because she and Nicholas were so mesmerized with each other, they began to walk over to the Leblancs together. Victoria had sat down on the ground and was fiddling with a little plastic thing that she'd spotted. Seeing her sister engrossed with something interesting, Katrine went over to find out what it was, and so Tash and Nicholas sat down together. It was a squash, but Tash and Nicholas didn't appear to notice.

Beside me, Celine did a little involuntary gasp, and I suddenly realized why. For the first time for years, maybe for the first time since the famous babysitting evening, Nicholas was sitting at a table with the Leblanc parents. I glanced over to the Lerois, and I could see that Monsieur Leroi was keeping an eye on what was going on over here. Celine, Sophie and I were making tons of "what-shall-we-do-now?" eye contact, but Tash was completely out of it. She was totally "gone" over Nicholas, and from what I could gather, the feeling was mutual.

"How are you, Nicholas? I haven't seen you for ages," said Celine, sounding very false, but obviously wanting to get to the point of this meeting as quickly as possible, before the moment was lost with nothing achieved.

"Very well," said Nicholas, coming back to earth suddenly, and then he looked round the table and looked a bit uncomfortable, as though he, too, had suddenly realized where he was.

"Did you have a good first evening?" Monsieur Leblanc enquired pleasantly of me. I decided to take a big gamble.

"Not particularly," I answered carefully, in my awful French, "Nicholas's friend made Sophie and me – " I suddenly realized I didn't know the French for drunk, so I mimed it, which I did by making my eyes go crossed and letting my head loll around. Madame Leblanc looked shocked, but Monsieur burst out laughing and provided me with the French word for drunk, which sounded like "Sue"!

"Nicholas's friend, eh?" said Monsieur Leblanc, and there was the teeniest hint of sarcasm in his voice, as though I'd said it was Nicholas's friend to protect Nicholas, but really we all knew that it had been Nicholas who had made us drunk.

"Thibault," said Sophie firmly. "I don't like him."

"Neither do I," said Nicholas, and everybody looked at him.

"You don't like your friend?" asked Tash in her most sympathetic voice.

He shook his head. "I have told him that he is no longer my friend."

"Good!" I couldn't help saying, because I felt pleased that Nicholas had come to his senses.

"Has he been your friend for long?" asked Madame Leblanc.

"Five years," said Nicholas. Then he said something in rapid French that I couldn't understand.

"What did you say?" Tash asked Nicholas, and he tried to repeat what he'd just said in English.

"This is not the first time he has done a wicked thing."

"What else has he done?" asked Tash, and I was surprised at her. Normally Tash wouldn't dream of asking such personal questions of a sixteen-year-old boy who she'd only just met.

There was a silence, during which Nicholas looked from Monsieur to Madame Leblanc and back again, as if deciding whether or not to answer Tash's question in their hearing. Nicholas then turned back to Tash and answered her question very slowly in English.

"He stole three videos and some money from Monsieur and Madame Leblanc, when he helped me look after their children once, two years ago. Then he told me that if ever I told anyone he would make sure I had a bad time at school from the other boys. So I told no one, because I was afraid. But after last night, I am filled with anger, and no longer afraid."

There was a gasp from Madame Leblanc, as Monsieur Leblanc rested his elbow on the table and rubbed his fingers thoughtfully on his forehead. Nicholas looked as though a huge weight had been lifted from his shoulders, and the worried look had left Tash's face, too. Monsieur and Madame Leblanc had obviously understood the slow English that Nicholas was speaking, but then Madame Leblanc spoke in French, but I think I understood correctly.

"We are so sorry, Nicholas," said Madame Leblanc, touching his arm. "I had no idea you had anyone with you at our house that evening."

"Henri," called Monsieur Leblanc across the picnic area, as he got to his feet. I couldn't understand what he said next. All I know is that he was striding over to Monsieur Leroi and the two men were shaking hands vigorously, and talking nineteen to the dozen, both at the same time, while Madame Leroi smiled delightedly, and Tash and I leant across the table and slapped each other's right hand, which is the Cafe Club gesture for '*Yessssss!*'

Chapter 11

Luce

I couldn't get that gorgeous boy out of my mind. Fancy me liking a boy who wears a necklace! I suddenly realized I'd stupidly not even thought to ask him his name. Now there was no chance of meeting up with him again, unless he went to that cafe every day. Maybe he did. A little walk in the early morning wouldn't be frowned upon by Monsieur and Madame Cardin, I felt sure. Which reminded me, I must give Madame Cardin her present from Tattlequack Farm.

"*Voila!*" I beamed at her as I handed the eggs over a minute later. She had her back to me and was making coffee. At the sound of my voice she spun round and gave me a big smile and the usual four kisses. I had forgotten that the French normally greet each other like this every single day.

"*Voila!*" I repeated, offering the eggs a little more forcefully.

"*Qu'est-ce que c'est?*" she asked.

"Eggs. *Oeufs*," I replied, still beaming away.

"*Un cadeau? Tu es tres gentille, Lucy.*"

127

She thought I was very kind. In fact, she gave me another kiss. Somehow I'd been expecting her to express great surprise and tell me how utterly ingenious I was, managing to buy eggs from a French farm just like that!

"*De la ferme*," I managed to say, which I hoped meant, "From the farm."

"*De la ferme?*" she repeated, with a huge question mark.

Aha! Now I had her interest. At that point, Jaimini, Michelle and Emma all came in together and asked in two languages where I'd been. So we all sat down and I told them the whole story, in a mixture of French and English, with a great deal of help from Michelle, and two French dictionaries, through which Jaimes and Emma flipped frantically every time we couldn't work out the French for something.

Shortly after I'd begun, Monsieur Cardin came in very quietly and sat down next to me at the table. I couldn't help but notice the glance that passed between Michelle and her mum, so I guessed that this was not his normal behaviour. Madame Cardin immediately jumped up and started to make fresh coffee and fetch more croissants, as if to try and keep her husband at the table with us for as long as possible.

When I got to the "farm" bit of the story, I could tell I'd got everybody really gripped, but Madame Cardin looked very worried indeed. Michelle said that the Alsatian dog at the farm is called Beau, which I suppose translates as "handsome". Apparently, Beau is the fiercest guard dog in the area, and nobody would ever dream of entering the farmyard when he's there on guard, unless accompanied by Monsieur or Madame Blanchard, the farmers.

"Are you sure?" Madame Cardin kept demanding of me. I couldn't work out if she was trying to establish whether I was sure we were all talking about the same farm and the same dog, or whether she thought I was making up the whole story about getting past the dog to provide a bit of breakfast entertainment. In the end I went to the cupboard where I'd seen her put the eggs, saw to my embarrassment that there were two dozen other eggs on the shelf with my present, tried to ignore this fact, and took my six eggs in the big box to the table, where everyone inspected it. Bingo! I *knew* I'd remembered correctly. Scribbled on the top in blue pen it said, "Blanchard", so now we all knew.

"You were very lucky to escape without harm," Michelle told me, and I felt a bit of a hero for a moment. The expression on Monsieur Cardin's face was a worried one, as though he was imagining what it would be like had I been mauled to death by the Alsatian. I broke into a big smile to try and cheer him up and he suddenly patted my hand, which made me feel very touched. Again that look passed between Michelle and her mother, only this time, Emma was in on the look, too.

"Guess what?" Jaimini suddenly said.

"What?"

"Andy phoned while you were out, and Jacques's parents have invited us all over for the day, the whole family. And she's also invited Laurette's family, the Lerois, and the Leblancs. Apparently there's some sort of bad feeling between the Lerois and the Leblancs that's been going on for about two years and the two families don't talk to each other at all, so it'll only be Fen with

Sophie, and Tash with Céline, at Jacques's. But isn't that brilliant? We're going to spend a day together!"

"Brilliant!" I agreed. I couldn't wait to tell everyone my "Beau and the heroine" story, nor could I wait to tell my friends my "beautiful French boy with necklace" story. I was really excited.

Two hours later we were rolling up the wide, sweeping drive to Jacques's place. It was breathtaking: in fact, I don't think I'd ever seen such a fantastic house. It was even more impressive than the Grange in Cableden, which is a huge mansion where Tash's mum used to work. Lucky old Andy and Leah!

Monsieur and Madame Cardin had turned down the offer to stay at Jacques's place because they both had a lot to do, they said, and Michelle was going out for the day with a friend, so Madame Cardin dropped off Emma, Jaimini and me. After four quick kisses with Jacques's mum, who looked like the kind of mother we all dream of having, away she drove, telling us she'd be back later. I could hear Marie-Jo (as I now knew Jacques's mum to be called) saying, "*Oui, oui, telephone,*" in a very throwaway sort of manner, so I guessed she was not making any plans in advance about when the day would be over.

As Madame Cardin pulled away, Andy, Laurette and Leah shot into view. They seemed miles away, at the far end of a wonderful garden, but it took Andy no time at all to get over to us, she's such a fast runner.

"Hi, you two," she called, then we all gave each other big hugs. After hugging Leah and Laurette, we suddenly all burst out laughing because we weren't sure where to start with our news. Marie-Jo had had to rush inside because the phone was ringing, but she came out at that point and gave Jaimini and me four kisses each. She was so smiley and friendly that I liked her instantly. Immediately after that we heard the sound of tyres crunching up the drive and we all registered at the same time that there were two cars, arriving one behind the other.

"Uh-oh!" I said. "Looks like the two enemy cars have mistimed their arrival."

Marie-Jo said something under her breath, which I guessed probably meant the same as I'd just said. We all just stood there looking spare, because no one wanted to take their eyes off the action. As soon as the two cars came to a standstill, out came Fen, Tash, Sophie and Celine from the same car. Personally I was so surprised that I couldn't even greet Tash and Fen properly because I wanted to see how the parents of the two families reacted. We'd all been led to believe that these two families wouldn't go within ten miles of each other, and yet here they were together – or was that just a horrible coincidence?

It was hard to see who was in the front of the two cars from where we were standing, but what happened next gave all of us a shock, because two men got out of the first car and two women out of the second. Of course, I'd only met Madame Leblanc before so I didn't actually know who these three other people were. Maybe it was Monsieur and Madame Leblanc and they'd brought a couple of completely different friends with them.

"*Mon dieu! Les deux familles sont ensemble!*" said Marie-Jo in a shocked whisper.

"What did she say?" we all demanded of Andy.

"It's the two families together," Andy quickly translated. "Don't stare," she added.

"It's all over. They're friends now," Fen informed us lightly, and Tash just smiled happily.

"*Qu'est-ce qu'elle dit?*" Marie-Jo whispered to Andy, while staring open-mouthed at the Leblancs and the Lerois, who were smiling as they made their way over to us.

"It's all over. They're friends now," Andy translated for Marie-Jo.

"*Mon dieu! Incroyable!*" breathed Marie-Jo, then she broke into a big smile and went towards the two women.

It seemed that once again Tash had worked her magic. We've always called her the peacemaker, but I reckon that particular bit of peace-making must have been her biggest feat yet. There were eleven of us all together, because Jacques had joined us, even though we were all girls. Celine's little sisters had been invited out for the day, Sophie's older brother Nicholas had said that he might join us later, and somewhere in the wonderful castle behind us was Bastien, Jacques's little brother, who was supposedly quite shy and withdrawn. Jacques said that Bastien would probably join us later, though.

The adults were sitting round Marie-Jo and Serge's swimming pool, all laughing and joking and talking at a hundred miles per hour. Sophie and Celine kept on going over to their parents and sitting with them, as though they couldn't believe that this was happening and they wanted to check that the two sets of parents were still friends. It was obvious to the rest of us that they were the best of friends, and Tash looked especially relieved and happy.

Fen and Tash had given us a blow-by-blow account of all the clever manoeuvres that the two of them, along with Celine and Sophie, had made to try and sort everything out. The rest of us had been totally gripped by the story, because it was better than any book I'd ever read! The same went for the "drunken evening" story. We all hung on to Fen's every word! Jaimini and I felt as though we led really boring lives because we hadn't got any such stories to tell. (My "Beau and the heroine" and "Boy with necklace" story would fall pretty flat after "English girls bring French feuding families together".) That Thibault made me feel sick. He'd caused nothing but trouble. The only good thing to come out of him spiking Fen and Sophie's drinks was that Nicholas had finally come to his senses and realized that he was strong enough to stand up to this monster, Thibault. *Good for Nicholas*, I thought.

"I hope Nicholas *does* come later," I said. "I'd really like to meet him."

"Do you think we will?" Tash asked Sophie.

"Probably not," Sophie replied, and I couldn't help noticing Tash looking rather crestfallen.

We'd already been for a swim earlier on and we were munching crisps and nuts and loads of other wonderful French *aperitifs* under a huge tree. We'd spread out a massive groundsheet and covered it with loads of towels. I felt as though I was in ecstasy. Well, almost in ecstasy. I was lying down on the edge of the ground sheet, where the sun shone, because I didn't feel like being in the shade, and I closed my eyes and thought, how could I ever be

LUCE

happier than this? I reckoned it would be impossible, and yet there was something insistently tapping away at the back of my mind, trying to remind me that there was just one ingredient missing that would have made me totally happy.

I suddenly sat up as I remembered. That boy. The one with the necklace. I wished he was here with me, then I *would* be one hundred per cent happy.

"What's up, Luce? Have you been lying on a tarantula?"

"What?"

"You shot up just then as though something had bitten you," Fen said, laughing. I looked round at the others and they were all grinning.

"No, I just remembered something, that's all. Nothing important. It's all right, you can stop staring and pass me one of those twister cheesy things."

"Tell them your adventure, Luce," said Jaimini.

"It'll sound boring compared with what you lot have been up to."

"Oh go on, Luce, tell us," said Leah.

So I told them the farm story in glorious technicolour because I got Andy to translate so I was able to exaggerate a bit to make it more breathtaking. And Emma helped a lot by continually interrupting me with some comment or other about the reputation of this big, fierce, go-for-the-throat dog. I found myself really enjoying spinning out the story and watching the expressions on the faces of everyone around me. When I got to the downpour and the cafe I felt a bit stupid with Jacques being there. I mean, he was a boy, and this was strictly girl talk, so I made it sound a bit more casual on purpose.

134

"I'd got no money because I'd spent it all on the eggs, and this bad-tempered waitress was waiting for me to order something. I'd absolutely no idea what on earth to do, although running out in the rain seemed quite attractive."

"Oh Luce, you are a nutcase," interrupted Tash.

"When suddenly I was rescued by this really nice boy. He bought me a coffee."

"Hold on, Luce. You don't like coffee!" Andy helpfully told everyone.

"Well, I do now," I informed her, going quickly back to my story. "We managed to communicate pretty well, actually, but then the rain stopped and I had to go."

"I thought you said that he had to go in the last version," Jaimini corrected me.

"Well, whatever. I can't remember now."

"That's a brilliant story," Tash said. "Did you get his name? Will you ever see him again, do you think?"

"How old was he?" asked Leah.

"Maybe Jacques will know him," said Andy. "Describe him."

"Well, he was about sixteen and he was wearing a black T-shirt and blue jeans, and he was really good-looking. Oh, and he was wearing a silver chain round his neck."

I'd tried to say it as casually as possible, because I didn't want anyone making fun of me, but for some reason or other, this seemed to have the effect of making the others want to quiz me even more than usual.

"You sound as though you really like him," Tash said, with her head tipped to one side, and a thoughtful smile on her face. She'd sussed me and I tried not to go red.

"Do you know him, Jacques?" Andy asked in French, then she said something else quite fast. I only caught the word "jeans", so I gathered she was translating for Jacques what I'd said the boy was wearing. In the middle of Andy's translation there was a sudden gasp from Sophie. She and Fen were staring at each other, eyes wide, looking horrified.

"What on earth's the matter?" asked Jaimini in English, and Emma and French, at the same moment.

"Nothing," said Fen.

"*Rien*," repeated Sophie.

"It can't be '*rien*'," I insisted. "What *is* the matter?"

"Nothing," said Fen, more firmly, and again her French echo copied. I was getting pretty exasperated by then. If it hadn't been for a huge splash and a scream, followed by a load of giggles from the adults, Fen wouldn't have been let off the hook so easily. But we couldn't resist rushing over to the pool to find out what had happened. What we saw when we got there was hilarious and sent us all rushing for our cameras. There were two plastic mats in the pool and Serge and Marie-Jo were having a competition to see who could stand up on their mat without falling into the pool. Marie-Jo was brilliant at it, and just stood there, perfectly balanced on her mat. She looked really nice in a blue and white swimsuit with her hair knotted on the top of her head. I wished I could look like her. She didn't put any effort into her appearance, and still she looked great, *and* she was about forty-five.

Serge was getting up very slowly indeed on to his mat, and had a look of grim determination on his face.

"*Cest la troisieme fois!*" called out Madame Leblanc.

"It is the third time," translated Monsieur Leroi.

Then we all waited with bated breath to see whether Serge would make it. Marie-Jo was still just standing there. I don't know how on earth she did it. Andy must have been wondering the very same thing because she called out something to her in French, which Marie-Jo answered, then turned to us and told us that she'd been practising during the night. That raised another laugh from everyone, but only a brief one because again our full attention was on Serge. He looked as though he was going to make it this time.

"*Vas-y, Serge,*" called Madame Leroi.

"Yeah, go on, Serge," said Andy under her breath.

He was almost upright, but his legs were really trembling with the effort of keeping his balance.

"*Bonjour,*" came a voice from behind us and we all turned to see who it was, including Serge, who promptly toppled into the pool at the most ungainly angle, which sent the rest of the adults into peals of laughter.

"Nicholas!" said Sophie, sounding pleased to see her brother.

"Nicholas!" called out Madame Leroi, waving happily across to her son.

"Nicholas!" called out Monsieur Leblanc, and immediately he came striding over with his hand outstretched to shake Nicholas's hand long before he got up to him.

Sophie excitedly introduced her brother to everyone, except Fen, Tash and Celine, who obviously knew him, then Nicholas went over to join the adults, mainly because he had no choice as Monsieur Leblanc's arm was firmly guiding him over to the bar by the pool. (I tell you, that place had everything!)

Madame Leblanc said something to her husband, which Andy translated for us. "She's trying to tell her husband tactfully that maybe Nicholas would rather be with us lot."

We decided to go and play *boules* on a gravelly bit of ground that had been specially put there for the game, because that's the sort of surface it needs. A minute or two later Nicholas came to join us. I noticed he went straight to Tash, and although I'm not the most observant person in the world, I also noticed the way they looked at each other. What a turn-up for the books! Tash looked truly besotted with this boy. I nudged Jaimini with my elbow, and she nodded and smiled then told me not to make it so obvious that we knew, so I whistled the French national anthem to distract anyone else who might also have noticed Tash and her gooey eyes.

For some unknown reason my whistling made everybody crack up. Goodness knows why, because I thought I was doing it really well.

"Hey! I'm a good whistler!" I protested, looking round.

"You're the best, Luce," said Andy, still grinning. "Come on, give us another tune."

The others were all egging me on, too, so I stood on a garden seat that was conveniently placed especially for impromptu performances like this, and whistled a medley of songs I knew. It didn't worry me in the slightest that I was making everyone laugh. In fact, in a way, I'm at my happiest when I'm making people laugh. Maybe I ought to consider comedy for a career? I'd never thought of that before. I was just arching my neck to amuse everybody even more as I struggled for a very high note when my wonderful performance was interrupted by another "*Bonjour*." I stopped mid-whistle because I recognized this voice. A tree was blocking my view from where I was standing on the bench, but the others could see who it was, and immediately it was obvious that they weren't happy.

A heavy silence hung over them all, and as the owner of the voice came into my view, two things happened. The first was that my knees turned to jelly so I could hardly stand on the bench any more, because this was *him*, my gorgeous French boy with the necklace. The second was that my pink face turned white because Nicholas had spoken just two words in a voice of steel, filled with a loathing and disgust that seemed to be mirrored in Fen's and Emma's eyes.

"*Au revoir, Thibault.*"

Chapter 12

Leah

Andy, Laurette and I were so excited when we heard that we were to have a day with all our friends, here at Jacques's place. Jacques didn't seem as excited as us, but that's because he's not as sociable as we are, and also I don't expect he wanted to hang out with a bunch of girls. I think his ideal day would have been spent just with Andy somewhere. I wondered whether Andy felt the same, whether she'd actually rather that Laurette and I went off and left her alone with Jacques. At one point I got all my courage together and asked her that very question, and she said, "No, of course not. It's not like that with Jacques. He's just my friend." I wasn't sure whether the answer was a hundred per cent truthful, but I didn't say any more.

Lisa turned out to be really nice and she was very happy to have a couple of English girls to talk to. She'd hated being away from Bastien, even though she'd been staying with some really good friends. She wanted to find out all about us, and the thing that she seemed most interested in was the fact that I played the violin and the piano. In true best-friend style, Andy made me out to be the most talented musician in the world, and Lisa wanted me to play something for her on Jacques's keyboard. I rather pathetically refused because the keyboard is quite different from the piano, and I know from bitter experience that I'm useless on it. (That's another story!) Bastien seemed very interested that I played the violin, too, and Lisa told us that he loved violin music and had got quite a few CDs of violin pieces. I thought this was really unusual for a boy of his age. Lisa spoke about Bastien very fondly, and I was beginning to realize what a big part she played in his life.

Marie-Jo said it was entirely up to Lisa what she did that day. She said that Lisa was very welcome to join in our fun day, but that if she preferred to go out for the day, that was fine, too, because Marie-Jo wasn't expecting her to be looking after Bastien as he would be spending the day with us and all the other families. In the end, after a lot of secret talking with Bastien, Lisa said she was going out, but that she wouldn't be late back, because she wanted to meet all the guests. Marie-Jo said something in rapid French at that point, with a big, sort-of-secretive smile for Lisa. I asked Andy what she'd said, and apparently it was something along the lines of, "Don't worry, you'll have another chance to meet the others because I've got a great day planned for us all." Of course, that got Andy and me very excited and intrigued.

Shortly before the others were due to arrive, when Andy, me and Laurette were about to play frisbee in the garden, we invited Bastien to join us, but he said he wanted to stay in his room and do a picture. I was dying to ask if I could stay and watch him do it, but I knew the answer would be no, so I left him to it. Jacques was reading the paper and said he'd join us later.

We'd been playing for about twenty minutes when the first car scrunched up the drive. Andy took off like a hare, and by the time Laurette and I got over there, Luce and Jaimini had been dropped off. It was absolutely wonderful to see them, and they were as excited as we were.

Various incredible things happened that day, and the first was the arrival of the Lerois and the Leblancs. We thought that the two families couldn't stand each other's guts, and that they never, ever communicated, but it turned out that there had been this massive make-up after two years of not speaking, and that Tash and Fen had been more than a bit instrumental in making it happen.

I was absolutely loving the day because everybody was so happy and relaxed. The adults were laughing and joking round the pool, and Luce told us about this typically Luce adventure that she'd had. Naturally enough for Luce, it involved a boy, only this time she seemed really smitten with him. I knew she thought she was making him out to be very unimportant, but that was the very thing that made me realize she was taken with him. This was not typical Luce, I can tell you.

Andy got Luce to describe the boy in case Jacques happened to know who it was, as Luce didn't even know his name. So Luce described what he was wearing, which was blue jeans, a black T-shirt, and a silver chain round his neck. I saw Fen's eyes widen as though she'd seen a ghost, and the next moment, when Andy had translated the description into French for Jacques, Sophie's eyes widened too, and the two of them exchanged a sort of horrified look. It suddenly occurred to me that perhaps Luce was describing Nicholas, Sophie's brother. But then Nicholas actually turned up and there was no cry of recognition from Luce, so I'd been wrong about thinking her knight in shining armour was him.

We had this great game of *boules* and right in the middle of it there was another "*Bonjour*" and we saw a boy of about Nicholas's age, dressed in blue jeans, a black T-shirt, and wearing a chain round his neck.

Luce jumped off the bench, from where she'd been accompanying our game with whistling, and the connection suddenly hit me like a splash of cold water on my face. This was Thibault, the hateful boy who was responsible for getting Fen and Sophie drunk. But this was also the boy with the necklace, who was the object of Luce's latest affections. I think the others must have made the same connection at exactly the same time as I did, because suddenly we were all watching Luce and, sure enough, her face turned sort of soft and embarrassed. I looked at Thibault and noticed that he was ignoring Nicholas and going towards Luce.

"*Lucy! Quelle surprise!*"

Then Monsieur Leroi came over and spoke in furious tones to Thibault. It was all too fast for any of us, except Andy, of course, to follow. We didn't really need a translation, though, because it was perfectly obvious that Monsieur Leroi was telling Thibault off for making Fen and Sophie drunk, and also for stealing the money and videos all that time ago. I caught the word "video", which is how I knew that that was what he was talking about.

Monsieur Leroi pointed aggressively towards the gate, presumably giving Thibault his marching orders, and after one long defiant look from Thibault, he obeyed Monsieur Leroi and strode off in a big temper. Luce had been looking from one to the other with an expression of complete concentration on her face, which showed how hard she had been trying to follow the conversation. When Thibault went striding off, she looked for a moment as though she was going to follow him, but I could see that Jaimini was keeping a careful eye on the situation, and when Thibault went, Jaimini gripped Luce's arm for a second, then put her arm round her shoulder briefly. This made all the fight go out of Luce, and she hung her head and looked so dejected that I felt really sorry for her.

Monsieur Leroi went back to the adults, who had been totally quiet during the exchange, and when their noisy laughter started up again, the rest of us kind of snapped out of our shocked state and all began talking at once. There followed a tremendous babble of French and English, with Andy in great demand for translation. Nicholas didn't want to talk about Thibault, though, so he and Tash went off together in the direction of the rose garden, which was the most wonderful-smelling place I think I'd ever come across. Poor Luce looked as though she was about to burst into tears, and Jaimini was quick to persuade her to come and look round the de Vallois estate. So off they went together, and I hoped like mad that Luce would feel better by the time she got back. Meanwhile, the rest of us carried on with our game of *boules*, but it wasn't the same after our interruption.

Maybe the adults sensed that we needed a bit of a boost

or something, because Marie-Jo called us over and started organizing ridiculous races in the pool. She mixed all the adults and children up in teams, but what she didn't realize was that Andy is very good at all sports, including swimming. Marie-Jo presumably put Andy with Jacques because she was putting a petite girl with a big strong boy to make the balance right, but in actual fact, she was creating the strongest possible combination, and after three or four races that Jacques and Andy won by miles the teams had to be thought out again. Luce and Jaimini came back during this, and a little later so did Tash and Nicholas, and for the next forty-five minutes we had the best fun of the day. I can't wait till my photos are developed, and everybody else's, because we all took loads of pictures and they should be really excellent.

"Marie-Jo wants to make an announcement," Andy suddenly called out, as she clapped her hands importantly. "Silence please for Marie-Jo's announcement!"

We all waited, and Marie-Jo began, in French, to say a few words at a time, and after each phrase Andy did the translation. The final announcement was really exciting, because Marie-Jo was proposing that we should all go to Disneyland, Paris, the very next day by train. It would only take about an hour and three quarters to get there, so we could come back the same day. The French lot were pretty excited, but we English were going absolutely crazy with excitement. This was like a dream come true. I'd always wanted to go to Disneyland, and the very next day I would be there! Fantastic! Luce was jumping up and down whooping, all signs of bereavement for the loss of Thibault apparently gone! For a little while we had to abandon the swimming races while everyone absorbed this brilliant piece of information and took their time calming down. Then we did a few more races, but we were all in such a silly mood that they didn't work so well and we had to abandon them.

At one point I glanced up and caught sight of a little face watching us from an upstairs window. It was Bastien. I'd forgotten all about him and I think the others had, too. I beckoned frantically to him to come and join us, but the moment he realized I'd seen him, his head popped out of view. I waited till there was a lull in the swimming races, when everyone was lying around lazily in the sun, then I crept off.

As I approached the house across the immaculate lawn, I kept an eye on all the windows. Bastien wasn't anywhere in sight. Inside the house it felt very cool and very peaceful. My bare feet didn't make a sound on the floorboards or on the carpeted staircases. Outside Bastien's room I stopped for a moment and listened. There wasn't any noise and I couldn't be certain whether he was still in his room or not.

"Bastien," I whispered, knocking gently on the door.

There was no reply. I tried again, but he still didn't answer, so I gently turned the handle and went in. Bastien was nowhere to be seen, but all over every available space on the floor, the bed, the desk and the chest of drawers were pictures and more pictures, all in the same style. I had to pick up the papers just to walk into the room. As I stared at the ones I'd picked up I felt chilled to the bone. These pictures were so full of ghosts and ghouls and creatures with wide staring eyes and horrible leering expressions that I shivered and let them drop from my hands. I turned to leave the room, but standing in the doorway was Bastien, looking at me accusingly as if to say, "How dare you come into my private room without asking permission." I tried to smile at him while pointing at his pictures and said, "*Tres bien, Bastien. Tres bien.*"

"*Tu ne les aimes pas bien?*" he asked, which he had to repeat slowly to allow me to work out what he meant.

"Yes, I do. I like them. Honestly," I quickly assured him in the best French I could muster. His face looked deflated, though, as though I'd said that I hated them. Someone else was behind Bastien at the door. It was Andy, thank goodness.

"Leah, what are you doing?" Her eyes went to the floor and she, too, was staring at the pictures, but being Andy she didn't react quite so obviously as I had done.

"Why do you you always do ghosts in your pictures?" I think she was asking him.

He replied in French and I asked Andy to translate.

"Because the ghosts are always in my head, and if I do not get them out on to paper I dream about them, which is very frightening."

"That's good, then," I said to Andy and she translated it with a smile. "May I look properly at them all?" Andy then asked Bastien, and he shook his head.

"We'd better go," Andy said to me, so we smiled and turned towards the open door.

Suddenly there were noisy footsteps on the staircase behind us and the sound of someone singing. I didn't recognize the singing voice and yet whoever it was was singing in English. A few seconds later Lisa came crashing into the room and Bastien ran straight over to her and gave her a big hug. He looked pleased to see her. What was strange was that Lisa was carrying a violin, which she handed to me.

"There," she said, swatting her hand over the bed casually to make the pictures flutter down to the floor. She then flopped on to the bed and lay down, with her fingers linked under the back of her head, as though she had just been on a crazy mission to find a violin and bring it back at all costs, and now she was exhausted. I jokingly said this to her, and she replied in a very matter-of-fact voice that this was actually what she *had* been doing.

"Bastien wanted to hear you play. He was desperate, actually. He gets like this sometimes. I can't tell you what a full-time job it is looking after such an artistic and gifted boy. But I've grown to understand him and his needs. That's why Marie-Jo doesn't want me to leave, because I manage to get through to Bastien where no one else can." She paused and smiled at Bastien. "So, can you play something, Leah?"

Bastien was sitting at his desk, waiting patiently.

"Yes, I expect so. I'm a bit rusty. I haven't practised for over a week."

"You'll be brilliant," Andy said to me.

"We'll leave them to it, shall we?" Lisa then said to Andy.

Andy looked a bit taken aback, but Lisa obviously knew what she was doing, so off they went, which left me, my violin, Bastien and a load of ghostly pictures.

I got the violin out of its case and tightened up the strings on the bow, then rubbed rosin all over it. I then put the violin under my chin and quickly tuned it. I hadn't even enquired where Lisa had got it. It felt different from mine, and sounded different, too. My violin at home in England was beautiful, with a lovely deep, dark tone. This one had a good tone, but not as nice as mine. I noticed that while I was tuning it, Bastien was getting out a clean pad of paper and a pencil, and I suddenly realized, from the way he was studying me, that he wanted to draw me while I was playing. I didn't mind. I thought I'd better play something soft and slow, though, because then I wouldn't move around so much. So for the next ten minutes I just kept playing. I finished one piece and went straight on to the next and the next. I can easily lose myself in my music and I suppose that's what I did, because I got a shock when I finally stopped and lowered the violin to hear the sound of thin clapping coming from outside the window. Bastien and I looked out together and there was everybody standing below, clapping up at me and smiling.

"*Formidable!*" cried Serge, which is the French for "terrific".

"*Extra!*" said Jacques, which means great.

"*Genial!*" said Nicholas, which I think means brilliant.

"Fantastic, Leah!" said Andy, and all the others said something or other, too, which made me feel like a famous violinist playing on the Queen's balcony to the crowds below. I had to smile. Then I looked round because I was suddenly aware that there were tearing noises going on behind me.

"Bastien! What are you doing? You can't do that! Lisa, Lisa! Come here. Quick! Bastien's tearing up all his pictures. There's going to be nothing left in a minute."

"Good!" she called back. "That's exactly what he's been wanting to do for ages. He hates those ghastly pictures. He just can't help doing them. He's got loads of other pictures that are tons better than the ghost ones, so don't worry."

She was smiling up at me but I wasn't convinced by her smile. She must have realized, because she said, "I'll come up." The others all drifted back to the pool, except for Marie-Jo and Serge, who exchanged anxious looks and had a quick discussion. I think they couldn't decide whether to let Lisa handle the situation or to try and sort it out themselves.

"Everything's fine, honestly," Lisa repeated when she got up to Bastien's room. "It was Bastien's idea to listen to you playing the violin. He knew from Jacques and Andy how good you are, and he loves music, especially the violin. You must have made him feel contented with your playing, otherwise he wouldn't have been able to tear up his pictures." Lisa turned to Bastien, "*N'est-ce pas, Bastien?*" she asked him, which meant, "Isn't that right, Bastien?"

He nodded as though he'd caught the general drift of what she'd been saying, then he showed us both his latest picture. It was of me, playing my violin, and it was absolutely incredible. It looked exactly like me. I just stared and stared at it, then told him I thought it was "*genial*", which was the word I'd heard Nicholas using earlier on.

Bastien's whole face broke into a smile and he handed me the picture. "*Pour vous*," he said.

"You *are* honoured," said Lisa. "I've never, ever known him give away one of his pictures. Not even to me."

And I *was* honoured. I really was.

Chapter 13

Jaimini

We had an absolutely wonderful day at Marie-Jo's, but the most fantastic thing was that the next day was going to be even better. Michelle hadn't come with us to Marie-Jo's, and when we got back to the Cardins' I sought her out and told her all that had happened. My French was getting better and Michelle's English was already very good, so our communication was fairly fast. When I told her about Luce and Thibault, she said she was glad that Luce seemed to have recovered from briefly fancying him because Thibault was thoroughly bad news.

When Michelle and I went downstairs it was to find Luce with Monsieur Cardin in the garden. He was relaxing in a deckchair listening to Luce as she chatted away in her funny French. Monsieur Cardin was leaning back with his eyes closed in the evening sun, and he had a smile on his face. Luce was such fantastic therapy for him, if only she'd known. I wasn't going to tell her, because I didn't want to spoil anything. She was in the process of trying to persuade him to come to Disneyland with us. Good old Luce! I noticed that she didn't succeed, however.

The plan was that Marie-Jo and Serge would be the only adults there, but Michelle was coming with us, as well as Katrine and Victoria. Monsieur and Madame Leblanc hadn't been at all sure about letting the younger girls go, but we assured them both that we'd all take care of them and that there was nothing to worry about, so finally they relented.

The following day I woke up very early because I was so excited. We met at the station, which was about an hour and forty minutes away from Disneyland. We practically filled up a whole carriage, and the journey passed quickly as we were all so keyed up. After we got to the main-line station in Paris, we had to take the underground to get to Disneyland. The most fantastic moment was coming up the escalator and being right there, instantly. It was like being in another world, full of colour and noise and crowds and excitement. We had a little booklet each, which clearly showed the sections into which Disneyland was split, like Fantasy Land and Adventure Land. It also listed the various rides. Luce, Andy and Fen wanted to go straight to Thunder Mountain, which was in the section called Frontier Land. In the end they persuaded us all to go. Katrine and Victoria wanted to go on a ride called Small World, so Marie-Jo and Serge went off with them, and they took Bastien, too. Apparently it was quite a breakthrough for Bastien to want to come to such a crowded place, because crowds faze him rather.

We all arranged to meet up outside a certain stall not too far from the Teacup ride at five o'clock. So off we went, and for the first time I noticed something that I kept on noticing all day long: that we'd formed pairs, and we kept in those pairs. Andy was with Jacques, Leah with Laurette, I was with Michelle, Luce was with Emma, Fen and Tash were together, and Sophie and Celine were together, too. Sometimes the pairs went into fours, and then it was Luce and Emma with Michelle and me, Andy and Jacques with Leah and Laurette, and Fen and Tash with Sophie and Celine.

Andy and Jacques got way ahead of us, and by the time Michelle and I arrived at the queue for Thunder Mountain, they were miles in front with Laurette and Leah not far behind. As it turned out, we didn't have to queue for more than about ten minutes, and then we all got buckled and barred into our seats. Luce was screaming before the ride had even begun. We had to go in threes for this ride, so Luce came with Michelle and me, which meant that I had to suffer that screaming in my ear for the whole ride. Emma went behind with Sophie and Celine. Fen, Tash and Leah were together, then Andy, Jacques and Laurette were at the front.

I understand why they call them white-knuckle rides now! I think I enjoyed it, but it's hard to tell because your whole body is flung all over the place and your stomach moves around as you plunge down the side of the mountain, then twist and turn back up again. I found that not only my stomach but my complete insides did cartwheels when we were plunged into darkness or turned practically upside down. I suppose if I went on the ride loads of times I'd get so used to it that I could concentrate on enjoying it, but for the first time, it was just a question of survival. Michelle felt the same.

Andy loved it and so did Jacques, and the last thing I

saw as Michelle and I went off with Luce and Emma to the Haunted House was Andy and Jacques standing in the queue to have another go. Jacques had his arm round Andy and she was leaning her head against his chest. They looked so lovely together, one so dark and tiny, and the other so big and blond. When I looked back a moment later, though, Jacques had moved his arm away and they were laughing hysterically about something. I really do think they have a brilliant friendship.

The Haunted House was excellent. We had to get into these little carriages in pairs, and then we went on the most spooky journey I think I've ever had, passing skeletons and ghosts and headless bodies that jumped out and brushed over us, nearly giving us heart failure. It made the ghost train at the fair seem like nothing.

Luce and Emma wanted to go through the whole journey again the moment we were back out in the open, but Michelle and I just felt like strolling around and taking in the atmosphere, so we did. The sun was strong and I felt completely relaxed and happy. Michelle was great company and we spent ages looking at all the souvenirs and postcards, sunglasses and T-shirts at the various stalls that were dotted about everywhere. I was determined to buy something before the day was over but I didn't want to be lugging stuff around, so I decided to leave it till later.

When we were sitting down eating ice-lollies on a little stone wall outside the entrance to one of the rides, a couple approached us with their camera. At first I thought they wanted one of us to take a picture of them, but then I realized that they wanted to take a picture of us!

"What's going on?" Michelle asked me. "Do you know these people?"

"No, I was wondering if you did," I replied. I turned to the man with the camera and was about to ask him why he wanted a photo when I realized he'd taken it. He smiled and thanked us, and the woman gave us a very big grateful sort of smile, then they went on their way. Michelle and I didn't know what on earth to make of it.

We got up and walked on to Fantasy Land, where we caught a brief glimpse of Marie-Jo and Serge with the two little girls at the start of the "Small World" ride.

"Shall we have a go on the Cup and Saucer ride?" Michelle asked me. We both watched the cups and saucers spinning round for a while, to see if this was really what we wanted to have a go at ourselves.

"How come some of them are going much more quickly than others?" I asked Michelle.

"Because there's a wheel in the middle that you can turn if you want to, which will make you go faster. You don't have to turn it if you don't want to, though."

"Oh great, let's go for it, then!" I said. As long as *I* could control the speed we were going at, I felt perfectly happy. Michelle felt the same, so when the cups and saucers had come to a standstill, we rushed straight into the rink and got into a beautiful pale-blue and gold one. We giggled excitedly and both felt a bit nervous.

Before the ride even started I became aware of someone in another cup staring at us. It was a man in his early twenties, I guessed. I ignored him and talked to Michelle, then looked round at the rest of the cups, which were rapidly filling up. When I looked back at the man who had been staring, a minute or so later, he was *still* staring, only this time he was whispering to his girlfriend. It was obvious they were talking about us, because the girl immediately looked over in our direction, then turned back to her boyfriend with an excited look on her face. After that, blow me if *she* didn't take out her camera and take a picture of the two of us! Michelle hadn't even been looking in the right direction.

"Don't look too obviously, but someone else is taking our pictures over there," I said to Michelle. "This is really weird."

"Where? Where?" But she never did see, because we were suddenly bombarded by two young French boys who leapt into our cup at the last minute. You see, each cup could seat four people and the ride didn't start till all the cups were full. Ours was the last to fill. Well, I didn't mind two other people being in the cup with us, but I *did* object to what they proceeded to do.

I guessed the boys were probably about eleven or twelve, and they obviously got a kick out of speed and terror because they couldn't keep their hands off the wheel, which made us go spinning more and more violently round and round, so we were not only spinning round the rink, we were also spinning round on our own axis. My neck ached from trying to stay rigid and I began to feel dizzy and sick. I couldn't turn to look at Michelle because I wasn't capable of moving a muscle, but I guessed she was probably in the same state as me, judging from the way she was gripping my hand.

"Tell them to stop!" I screamed in terror.

"*Arretez! Arretez!*" she yelled at the boys, but they were having the time of their lives and just ignored her.

The relief when that ride was over was indescribable. Michelle and I stumbled away on our shaky legs, then went to find the nearest place where we could sit down and have a Coke. It took us about ten minutes to recover. Then – you won't believe this – somebody was taking our picture for the third time.

"This is unreal!" said Michelle.

"Where did you pick up that expression?" I asked her, because her English was getting really impressive.

"From Luce," she replied with a grin, and I realized that it was true. Luce did use that expression a lot.

We both glanced around to check that we were free from photographers, then I giggled and said, "I suppose this is how famous people must feel. They're always having to look over their shoulders in case someone's trying to take their picture."

"That's it! Of course," said Michelle, and she took out a little hand mirror from her rucksack. "We must look like someone famous."

We both peered into the little mirror, but it was impossible to see both our reflections at the same time unless we held the mirror about a metre away, which was also impossible, so we took turns. After about twenty seconds of careful study of our faces Michelle laughed and put the mirror away, because she said she didn't want people to think we were the vainest girls in the country. We'd almost finished our Cokes and were about to move on when a little girl appeared at my side and just stood there, grinning at us.

"Hello," I said.

"*Bonjour*," said Michelle, who looked as baffled as I felt.

The little girl said something very softly to Michelle in French, and comprehension dawned on Michelle's face.

"What? What did she say?" I demanded impatiently.

"She wants our autograph. She thinks we're Shanine and Rianna! You know, the two-girl singing group who have suddenly made it big in France?"

I was ashamed to say I'd never even heard of them, but I was very curious to know what they looked like. Michelle explained to the little girl that though we looked like her idols, she was sorry but we weren't them. The little girl went away looking utterly dejected, and I got the impression that she didn't actually believe Michelle, so we quickly left the cafe before the girl's mother could accost us and demand that we sign autographs for her daughter.

"This is amazing," said Michelle as we walked along. "Can you feel people staring at us?"

I knew what she meant. It was weird. Part of me liked the attention, but the other part of me felt quite alarmed by it!

Chapter 14

Tash

When I heard that Nicholas wasn't coming to Disneyland with us I could have burst into tears. It wasn't so much that I was desperate to have him by my side twenty-four hours a day, more that I'd thought he wanted to be with me as much as I wanted to be with him, and now I'd got the absolute proof that he didn't, I felt rejected.

Fen was being really sweet to me. I think she guessed how I must be feeling and was trying to cheer me up. I decided to snap out of my silly mood and just enjoy myself – after all, it wasn't every day that I did something as wonderful as going to Disneyland. Fen and I stuck together all the time.

The first thing we did was go on Thunder Mountain, which is supposed to be the most scary ride of all. When we were standing in the queue I had a moment of total panic where I nearly ran straight out again, because I suddenly realized that I'd completely forgotten to take my epilepsy tablet that morning, but I quickly pulled myself together because now I've got my medication sorted out,

I knew it wouldn't make any difference just missing one tablet. Occasionally if epileptics get very cold, very tired, or very tense, it can bring on a fit or an absence, but not necessarily. I knew that really, there was nothing to worry about, because it was a hot day, I wasn't tired and I wasn't tense. Also I'd got Fen beside me. She's the only person in the world, apart from my family, my doctor and the teachers at school, who knows about my condition.

Thunder Mountain was absolutely incredible. I felt as though I was flying and diving and breaking the speed barrier. I really loved it, and when the other two were screaming, and Luce's screams were penetrating the whole of Disneyland, *I* was actually laughing! I couldn't wait to tell Mum and Danny about it. Jacques and Andy went back for another go afterwards, and I felt tempted to do the same, but as Fen said, there were tons of other brilliant rides to try out.

We'd all arranged to meet up together at an appointed place after an hour and forty minutes, so until that time everybody was free to go wherever they wanted, though Serge did say we weren't allowed to wander round on our own. We had to stick with at least one other person. Jaimini and Michelle went to the Haunted House, but Fen and I were desperate to go to the Discovery section, which was the sort of science-fiction, futuristic bit. We had a great time heading for a particular rocket ride that we both wanted to go on. The reason it was great was because along the way, we couldn't resist having a go on a few other rides too.

Then we stopped to have a burger and a drink. We kept on wondering if we'd see any of the others during the day, but we only saw Jaimini and Michelle. They were sitting in one of those teacup things from Alice in Wonderland. We tried to attract their attention but they were whispering together about something. I thought how pretty they looked with their faces so close together, both with shiny black hair and big black eyes.

The rocket ride was better than we could have imagined, and Fen and I had a great time pushing forward the lever that sent our particular rocket soaring up higher than the others for a few seconds. When we dared to look round we could see so much of Disneyland spread out below us and I kept on thinking what a brilliant day it was – probably one of the best in my life.

Apart from Thunder Mountain, the only thing we had to queue for ages for was a 3D Michael Jackson film. To watch the film all the audience were given special 3D glasses, and wearing these, you felt as though you were actually *in* the film, especially when creatures appeared to come flying out at you, right into your face. I even started batting my hand about in front of my eyes as though there really was something buzzing around my head. Fen caught me doing it and couldn't stop giggling, to my great embarrassment. Michael Jackson sang and danced absolutely brilliantly, and Fen and I kept on and on talking about the film long after we'd chucked our 3D glasses into this huge box with everybody else's. But as we emerged from the studio and the daylight hit us, we realized with a horrible shock that we'd forgotten all about the time.

"Omigod!" said Fen, looking at her watch. "It's five o'clock!"

"Omigod!" I agreed. "All the others'll be waiting for

us. I bet they'll be really cursing us for making them hang about in this heat. Quick! Run!"

So we quickly studied our little plan of the layout, to make sure we were going in the right direction – because it's easy to lose your way unless you're sure where you're going – then we set off at a gallop back to the meeting place. It took us ten minutes of jogging to get there, and we could clearly see as we approached that everybody was already there except Leah and Laurette.

"At least we're not the very last," Fen said.

"Unless Laurette and Leah have arrived and gone again," I answered, feeling guilty.

"No, there's Laurette! Look!" said Fen breathlessly.

I couldn't answer because I was even more breathless than she was, as I'm not such a good runner. Marie-Jo was the first to spot us and she looked very relieved to see us, and gave us a nice smile, which instantly made us feel better.

"*Nous sommes desolees*," Fen and I said in unison. We'd worked hard to remember that word "*desole*", which means really sorry. But as we stood there, panting and guilty, it gradually dawned on us that Marie-Jo didn't seem that bothered about us, and neither did any of the others.

"Leah's missing," said Andy quietly.

"Leah's missing! Oh no!" That explained why everyone had looked almost disappointed to see us. They obviously hoped we'd have Leah with us. "But I thought she was with Laurette."

"She was. Laurette can't understand it. Apparently one minute Leah was right behind her and the next minute she'd just vanished into thin air. They were only about twenty-five metres from this very spot, and Laurette stayed right where she was for a good five minutes when she discovered that Leah had vanished, then she came here to see whether Leah had already come to the meeting place."

"When did this happen?" I asked.

"About half an hour ago," Andy told us.

"Poor Laurette must have been so worried," I said. "But Leah can't be far away, can she?" I whispered to Fen. She didn't reply, so I turned back to Andy. "What's Marie-Jo going to do?"

"She wants to wait another thirty minutes to see if Leah turns up. She reckons there may be a perfectly simple explanation."

"Yeah, perhaps she just lost track of the time like we did," said Fen.

But Andy didn't look convinced. "I'm going to suggest to Marie-Jo that she and Serge stay here with Katrine, Victoria and Bastien, and the rest of us all go off in pairs and search for her. I feel so helpless just standing here."

Marie-Jo agreed to Andy's suggestion, so we all took a different area to search.

"Don't be longer than thirty minutes," said Serge. "Thirty minutes, OK?"

Chapter 15

Andy

Until five minutes ago, this was my dream day. Jacques and I are getting closer and closer, and I'm already dreading leaving him when we all go back to England. He doesn't want me to go either, which makes me feel good. I still don't know if we're boyfriend and girlfriend or just good friends. All I know is that I don't want anything to get in the way of our friendship. I don't think he fancies me or anything. I'm not like the others. I feel too little to be anyone's girlfriend, especially anyone like Jacques, who's so big.

Thunder Mountain was fantastic. Jacques and I had three goes on it altogether. We clung to each other and screamed and laughed and adored every single stomach-turning dip and dive and whiz and zoom. After that we sat down with an ice-cream each and talked for a while, as well as taking three pictures each of each other. I've always despised girls who have pictures of boys in their pencil cases and their school files, but I'd already planned to stick Jacques's photo in the inside cover of my file. I must be going really soppy.

I was as keen as Jacques was to go on as many rides as possible in the time we had, so between rides we moved on very quickly to the next. We completely forgot to eat because we were so absorbed in having fun and being with each other, but finally, when my stomach was rumbling so loudly that it was getting embarrassing, we sat down and had a baguette, and the day carried on getting better and better.

Jacques and I were first to arrive at our meeting place, and I hoped everyone would get there quickly so we could all go off again and have another big fun-packed session. Jaimini and Michelle turned up at the same time as Serge and Marie-Jo, with the two very excited little sisters of Sophie, and Bastien. The eight of us then chatted happily about our adventures, while waiting for the others to arrive. We heard about how people kept taking Michelle and Jaimini's photo, thinking they were famous. It was unbelievable. I'd seen a picture of Shanine and Rianna in a magazine that Laurette had been reading, and I had to admit that Jaimes and Michelle were stunningly similar. Jaimini looks older than thirteen and I think Shanine and Rianna are about sixteen, so it was no wonder people mistook them so easily, seeing both of them together like that. Thank goodness it wasn't Luce, or we'd never have heard the end of it!

Just as I was having that thought, Luce and Emma appeared. Jaimini seemed quite relieved to see them. I think she takes on a kind of motherly role where Luce is concerned, and always feels as though she's responsible for her. Poor old Jaimes.

A minute later Sophie and Celine showed up, so we

165

were just waiting for Fen and Tash, and Laurette and Leah. The next minute Laurette turned up, but something was wrong. Her face was pale and had an anxious look.

"Have you seen Leah anywhere?" she asked me.

"No, I thought she was with you."

"We got separated. I don't know how on earth it happened. One minute she was behind me, the next she was nowhere to be seen. I stayed in the same spot for ages so that she'd find me easily if she'd just nipped off to get something, but in the end, when she didn't come back, I thought I'd better come to the meeting place. That was half an hour ago. I'm getting worried now."

I asked Marie-Jo what she thought we ought to do and she told me not to worry just yet. "I'm sure Leah will suddenly appear, Andy. Let's give her a bit longer. She may be with Fen and Tash."

"How much longer do you think we ought to give her?"

"Well, maybe half an hour?"

At that moment Fen and Tash came rushing over, looking and sounding really guilty and full of apologies. Even though I was worried about Leah, I couldn't help smiling at the way they both said, "*Nous sommes desolees*," in unison, as though they'd been rehearsing it for weeks.

After another minute or two I couldn't bear it any longer and I suggested to Marie-Jo that we all go off to different areas and search for Leah. Marie-Jo agreed that this was probably a good idea. She said that she and Serge would stay at the meeting place with Katrine, Victoria and Bastien, while the rest of us went on the search. Serge stressed that we were to be no longer than thirty minutes.

"Will they be all right here?" Tash asked me, in her

usual thoughtful way. "I can stay with the little ones, if Marie-Jo and Serge want to join in the search."

Marie-Jo told me to tell Tash it was sweet of her to offer, but that Serge would go and buy ice-creams and drinks for all five of them, and they'd be fine. The cheese baguette I'd eaten suddenly seemed to be weighing me down because I was so worried about Leah being missing.

The area that Jacques and I were searching was round the Pirates of the Caribbean. "This is going to be impossible," said Jacques. "We'll never find her. Disneyland is huge and she could be on one of the rides, couldn't she?"

"We'd be wasting time if we went on the rides looking for her, Jacques. We've only got half an hour."

"Let's just scan this whole section as fast as we can, then." So that was what we did, but as the half-hour wore on, without any sign of Leah, I became more and more depressed. I just prayed that one of the others had been in luck.

Fen

At first I thought I was going to be spending the whole time at Disneyland trying to cheer up Tash because she so badly wanted Nicholas to be there, but as it happened she recovered very quickly and we started to have a wonderful day. The only trouble was that we didn't think ahead and plan it properly. We just went on ride after ride, and hadn't a clue whereabouts we were half the time! Eventually we turned up in the Discovery section and had a fantastic time on the Rockets, zooming over the crowds. I felt like a huge golden eagle. It was so wonderful up there.

After that we saw a 3D Michael Jackson film, which seemed a good idea at the time, but it was this that made us late back to join the others. When we realized how late we were, we ran really hard all the way back. The only conversation we had during that frantic run was a discussion about what the French for "We're really sorry" was. Tash and I scraped the bottom of our memories and came up with the word "*desole*". We were so proud of ourselves to have remembered this word, and we practised saying "*Nous sommes desolees*" in preparation for meeting up with Marie-Jo.

Surprisingly, she didn't seem all that bothered. Or more to the point, it was as though she was looking for someone else and not us. It only took a minute to discover that Leah was missing. Laurette and she had somehow got split up. Andy wanted to go off and search for her straight away, so Marie-Jo and Serge said they would stay at the meeting place with the younger ones, while the rest of us went off in pairs.

Tash and I were bound for Frontier Land where Thunder Mountain and Phantom Manor are. We both felt starving hungry but didn't dare waste a second of the precious half-hour buying ice-creams or anything else to eat.

"As soon as we find her we can get something," I said to Tash. It worried me that she looked so wilting and worn out. "Are you feeling OK, Tash?"

"Yeah, I'm fine. Just hot and tired, and I can't help worrying about Leah."

"Me too."

The queue for Thunder Mountain was miles longer at this time of day and we scanned as much as we could see, but there was no sign of anyone with long blonde hair.

"What if we don't *ever* find her?" asked Tash.

"I'm sure we will. Anyway, let's cross that bridge when we come to it," I replied. In truth, I had been worrying about the very same thing, but Tash looked so pale and awful that I didn't want to get her worrying any more than necessary. "I bet Andy will have found her by now, and we'll get back to the meeting place and find everyone rejoicing and happy."

"Hm," was Tash's only reply. Not a very convincing one.

As we came round the bend on the other side of Thunder Mountain, I thought I saw someone just like Leah walking along looking lost. This girl was too far away for me to shout out to, though.

"Look, Tash! Over there! Do you think that's Leah?"

"Where?"

"Next to that Mickey Mouse. Can you see?"

She was dodging to left and right and jumping up to try and see over the crowds, but obviously couldn't, and a moment later I'd lost sight of the blonde girl, too.

"Let's run. We might be able to catch her up." So we did. It wasn't easy because there were people in the way the whole time, but I felt that we were making quite good progress and must have narrowed the gap considerably, but I still couldn't see any long blonde hair. We both stood on a little wall and scoured the crowd carefully. I had my hand over my eyes to shield them from the sun.

Suddenly, I caught sight of her face. It was definitely Leah. There was no mistake.

"Tash! Tash! I've seen her. I swear it's her. Quick!"

I turned to Tash, but she'd got down from the wall. "Come on, Tash."

And then I realized. Tash's eyes were completely glazed over. Her head had lolled to one side and her mouth had dropped open. She was having an absence. I gulped and kept my eyes on her for just two seconds before allowing my gaze to go back to the crowd. I could still see Leah but she was walking away from us. I had to think quickly. What should I do? Should I try and sit Tash down on the wall and run off faster than lightning to try and attract Leah's attention? No, I couldn't do that. Tash would come round and find that I wasn't there. She wouldn't have any memory of her absence. She'd start looking for me, and she'd probably get lost herself. Or, worse still, some well-meaning person might come along and start interfering, carting Tash off for medical help or something. No, I couldn't leave her. Leah was almost out of sight by now. On an impulse I took a deep breath and yelled at the top of my voice, "Le-ah!"

I was aware that people around me thought I was totally mad and very uncouth, but I didn't care. Screwing up my lungs I tried again, but it was no good, she was completely out of sight. I studied Tash carefully and saw that she was coming round. I mustn't rush her, though. I knew I had to let her take her time. There was no way I could leave her yet, and it looked as though I'd lost my chance with Leah.

Leah

Thunder Mountain terrified me, but I didn't let on to anyone. I pretended I was enjoying it just as much as the others, but I couldn't even scream I was so terrified. I don't think anyone realized, though, because for one thing, Luce's screams were loud enough for all of us!

Andy and Jacques wanted to go through the torture a second time, and I think Laurette would probably have quite liked the idea as well, but I persuaded her that there were loads of other things we could do, so we went off together. I was determined to put as much space between us and Thunder Mountain as possible, so we headed for Discovery Land, which had a fantastic Michael Jackson film that you watch through special glasses that make it look as though it's in 3D. Laurette had other ideas, however. She wanted to go on Space Mountain and she assured me that I'd absolutely love it, so we joined the queue and I began to feel uneasy again, because I thought this was probably a case of "out of the frying pan into the fire". Anyway, I was in the queue and would have felt a fool if I'd chickened out at the last minute.

If anything, it was worse than Thunder Mountain. Laurette thought it was fantastic, but I felt utterly sick. It was the scariest, darkest, fastest ride through space you can imagine. My heart missed a beat every time we nearly ran into a planet, and in the end I just shut my eyes, which made me feel dizzy, but at least that was better than feeling scared and ill.

"Did you like it?" Laurette asked me as we walked away.

"Yeah, great," I lied. Surely she could see that my face was green?

"Shall we have an ice-cream?"

"I'm not hungry."

So Laurette had an ice-cream and I tried to hang on to my insides while we strolled around admiring the wonderful sights, deciding what to do next. I was hoping that Laurette's ice-cream would take her ages to eat so that we didn't have to do anything straight away. Maybe I should have stayed with Marie-Jo and Serge, than I could have done nice, safe things for young children, like the Peter Pan ride. That looked good fun.

"Shall we go on the Peter Pan ride?" I suggested to Laurette, and she wrinkled up her nose as though I'd suggested going home.

In the end I just told Laurette straight out that I couldn't cope with all the scary rides that most normal people loved. She laughed and said it didn't matter one little bit. So we compromised and went on a mixture of "safe" rides for me and scary rides for Laurette. The safe rides we went on together, but I left Laurette to get on with it on her own for the scary ones!

It was while we were waiting to go on a ride that I thought I heard someone call out my name, so I turned to see where the voice had come from. Maybe there was more than one Leah, I thought. When I turned back, Laurette had moved a few steps further forward and was still dodging this way and that trying to see something.

"Leah! Over here!" There it was again. The voice was

French, even though the words were English. It had quite a strong accent. This time it sounded a little closer and a little more urgent. I turned again, and saw a boy about the same age as Nicholas smiling and beckoning to me. Maybe it *was* Nicholas. I was wearing sunglasses and it was hard to tell. He definitely seemed to know me, whoever he was. I touched my chest as if to say, "Do you mean me?" and he nodded and beckoned me very urgently this time, so I went over to him to see what he wanted. I was pretty sure by now that it wasn't Nicholas, but it was someone very similar-looking.

"Over here," he said, striding away but turning to make sure I was following. I couldn't go much further or I'd lose Laurette.

"What do you want?" I called.

"Someone wants you," he said, in his very strong accent.

"Where?"

"Here."

He had stopped at last. I caught him up with a sick feeling in the pit of my stomach. Aline was standing there, grinning at me triumphantly.

"Leave me alone," I said, turning to go back to try and find Laurette, but I felt a painful tug on my arm and realized that another boy, also about sixteen, had grasped my arm and wasn't letting me go.

"Let go of me," I cried, tugging without success. Some people were passing us at that moment and I thought they would have realized that I was in a state, but they all just ignored me. They probably thought this was my brother or something and that we were having a friendly tussle.

"What do you want?" I asked Aline.

"She wants to show you something," said the boy with the strong accent.

"What?"

"Come."

The other boy was still gripping my arm so I had no choice. His grip was so hard that it hurt. The look on his face was the most frightening thing, though, because his expression was so cold and threatening. As we walked along, the anger that I had felt gave way to a hopeless, horrible panic. I'd already lost my bearings. I'd never find my way back on my own.

After about five minutes, we came to a ride called the Pirates of the Caribbean. The others were pulling me along towards the queue. People were behind us, and after a while I realized we were going further and further underground. I was shaking uncontrollably and could hardly hold back my tears, but then something even worse happened. I began to feel claustrophobic. If I'd been with the others I wouldn't have minded at all, but with these two horrible boys and the still-grinning Aline, I could feel mounting panic joining my terror.

My watch showed me that I was already late for our meeting, and that made me worry even more, because I knew all the others would be filled with alarm, especially Andy. I tried to keep a picture of Andy in my head. It somehow helped, because it reminded me that if Andy had been in this position, she wouldn't have got totally wimpish like me. She'd be keeping calm and figuring out what to do. I tried to get focused and do the same. After all, all I had to do was to get through the ride, then I could run away and escape from the others, and if they tried to grab me again I'd get someone's help. Even if I had to make a big scene, I would do it. Anything to get away.

The ride was horrific. It made Space Mountain and Thunder Mountain seem like the best moments of my life. At least I'd been in nice, safe company then. I would have given anything to set eyes on Laurette at that moment. The ride was in a boat and the automatons looked so incredibly lifelike that you really felt as though you were moving through the dingy, squalid world of pirates. The voices all around seemed to be coming directly from the pirates. I shrivelled into the corner of the boat and did my best to imagine I was Andy, but when I thought about her it just made me more anxious and depressed than ever. Cramped into the darkness I gave in and let silent tears run down my face, which made my throat hurt terribly.

At last the awful experience came to an end. As we mounted the steps, my heart was beating and my knees were trembling but I was trying with all my might to get my self-control back and to brace myself for a fast escape.

"Just focus on Andy," I told myself, and keep that determination going. The other three were talking and laughing more loudly than anyone else around us. They sounded really hard and thuggish to me. I hated having to be with them. No one was holding my arm, though, and we were almost out in the open again. "Right, this is it," I told myself, still focusing on Andy. It was amazing – it was almost as though she was propelling me forwards.

The very second the sunlight hit me I took to my heels

and ran. I'd chosen the perfect moment, because the two boys were racing each other and doing an imitation of one of the pirates who'd been swinging on a rope above the water, while Aline laughed at them.

"*Jean, elle est partie!*" I heard her shrill voice urgently warning the others that I'd escaped. I didn't even turn round, just ran blindly towards the nearest bend in an attempt to lose them.

Chapter 16

Andy

"**P**lease let someone have found her, please let someone have found her," I said to myself all the way back to Marie-Jo and Serge. Again we were the first back, and they both gave us searching, enquiring looks as soon as they saw us coming into view.

"Any luck?"

Jacques and I shook our heads. I could see Jaimini and Michelle coming back too, with Laurette. Jaimini came running up to see if Leah had been found. I saw the disappointment on everyone's faces change to hope very quickly as we all realized together that there were still Fen and Tash, Celine and Sophie, and Luce and Emma to come back yet. Two minutes later they were all back, and I felt utterly hopeless.

"What are we going to do?" Tash asked miserably.

"I'm sure I can find her," I said.

"But you've tried, Andy," said Serge.

"No, I'm really sure, this time. I want to go on my own. I know what I'm doing. I won't get lost. Please let me try. I just know I can do it."

I'd no idea what it was that had suddenly sparked me into action, but in one second flat I had changed from feeling hopeless to feeling absolutely positive and determined.

"Andy's often quite intuitive," Jaimini said to Michelle, but even Michelle's good English wasn't up to understanding this word. So I translated for Michelle what Jaimini had said, and it was Michelle who persuaded Serge and Marie-Jo to let me have one more chance. I didn't wait a second longer than necessary, and as I hared off, the last thing I heard was Serge telling me to be back in twenty minutes.

"You lot go on another ride," I called out. "I'll be OK, honestly." I hoped that they would go on another ride. Those poor little Leblanc girls must have been so bored. As I ran along I had the strong feeling that I was heading in the right direction. I was going back to the Pirates of the Caribbean. When I'd been there with Jacques I'd felt sure that *we* would be the two who would find Leah, and now I was back there, I felt it again. I just stood there and watched the people emerging into the daylight. "Come on, Leah. I know you're in there," I said to myself, and then suddenly I spotted her. My instinct was to go belting over to her, but I stopped myself when I saw the look on her face. She looked more scared than I thought I'd seen her for a long time, but she looked determined, too.

And then I saw why. Aline was right beside her with a couple of hard-looking older boys. The girl just *had* to be at the bottom of this, didn't she? I wanted to kill her.

Suddenly Leah made a bolt for it. The two boys were mucking about and didn't notice her going, until Aline's nasty shrill voice announced to the whole of Disneyland that Leah had fled. I followed Leah round the bend, but then I couldn't see her. She was making an incredibly good escape, choosing a route where she could quickly get out of sight then find a hiding place.

"Andy! Over here!"

"Leah! Are you all right?"

I joined her on the other side of a souvenir stall, and saw that she was shaking.

"Have I made everybody cross with me?" she asked.

"No, just worried. We must get straight back."

"I'm not going anywhere until I'm certain I'm not being followed. It's been awful, Andy. Aline got these two thugs to lure me away, then they wouldn't let me go. One of them kept a grip on my arm the whole time. They forced me to go on the Pirates of the Caribbean and I hated it because I knew you'd all be worrying and cross and I couldn't get away. I just kept concentrating on you and what you would do the whole time. That's how I got away from them. I took all my courage in both hands and just ran."

"I saw you. I was impressed."

"You saw me?"

"Yes. We've all been searching for you in pairs, but then I just had to go back on my own. I knew I'd find you. It was almost as though you were calling to me and telling me where to come. Weird!"

At that moment I spotted Aline and the two boys way over to our left and walking away from us.

"Come on, Leah. They're right over there. Let's get back to the others."

So we jogged back, and as we came into view of the meeting place I saw that Marie-Jo and Serge had done what I'd suggested and gone off with Katrine, Victoria and Bastien, thank goodness. Everyone else was there, though, and Jaimini was the first to spot us.

"Andy! Leah! Brilliant!"

Then they all came surging forwards to meet us and to overwhelm poor old Leah with questions. Tash gave Leah a big hug, which made Leah look as though she was about to burst into tears. Then Marie-Jo and Serge came rushing over, back from one of the rides, and so Leah had to tell the whole story again. Serge looked absolutely furious and wanted to track down Aline and the two thugs immediately, but Marie-Jo persuaded him that it would be wasting our time, and would also be sinking to their level.

"These things have a way of sorting themselves out," she said. "Come on, let's enjoy the rest of our day."

So we did, and when we all compared notes on the train going home, everybody agreed that the last part was the best part. There were no further sightings of Aline and Co. We stayed till late and had a huge junky meal together, then watched this incredible procession. The lights were amazing. Bastien was mesmerized by them, because he loved the colours and the designs that the lights were forming. The costumes and the carriages were out of this world, and we had the most fantastic view. At first we were stuck behind this tall family, but then they suddenly looked at their watches and decided that they'd better go, so we just moved forwards into their places. Wonderful!

Luce

The day after Disneyland I lay in bed in the morning and thought through all that had happened. It really had been an incredible day. Emma and I had been on more rides than anyone else. I know that for a fact because we all counted up on the train going home. I'd spent all my money on souvenirs for Mum and Terry and the terrible twins, as well as a few little things for myself. When I laid everything out on my bed at Emma's, though, I thought it looked like a tacky load of junk, especially when it was beside the tasteful little selection of stuff Jaimini had bought. Why am I so impulsive? Why don't I think before I do things, and consider everything a bit more carefully?

At breakfast time, the entire Cardin family had a good laugh at my attempts to describe the day to Monsieur Cardin. Michelle had to keep correcting me because I used lots of wrong words. At least I made an effort, which was more than some people did. I'd been trying to explain about the floats in the procession and, naturally enough, I didn't know the French for float. I mean, you wouldn't, would you, if you were only thirteen? So I thought to myself, *OK, Luce, what do they look like?* and I decided they looked a bit like chariots, so I did a quick adaptation to a French pronunciation of the word, which is like this, *sha-ree-o*, then mentioned the *"belles dames"* or beautiful ladies who were riding along in them, and that's when Monsieur Cardin clutched his stomach and rocked with mirth, with Madame, Michelle and Emma not far behind on the laughter scale.

"What?" I demanded indignantly. "What's wrong with that?"

Michelle was the first to recover and she managed to explain through her spluttery left-over giggles that "*un chariot*" is a supermarket trolley, so then that sent Jaimini rolling in the aisles. Honestly, anyone would think I'd cracked the joke of the century. I mean, what's so funny about a beautiful lady riding along in a procession in a supermarket trolley? Exactly. Nothing.

Thank goodness the joke finally fizzled out when there came a knock at the door, and in walked a man of about sixty. He was dressed in old clothes and he smelt of farm, if you know what I mean. Monsieur Cardin seemed very pleased to see him, and the farm man seemed very surprised to see Monsieur Cardin. Well, maybe not surprised to see him, but certainly surprised to see him laughing at the breakfast table. I had thought a lot about Monsieur Cardin, and I knew that before I came he'd had something wrong with him. He acted like he was recovering from an illness, or maybe he'd had some sort of massive fall out with his family or something. All I knew was that he had that same sort of "distant" nature that Andy's dad did. There was only one way to cope with Andy's dad, and that was to act completely normally, which in my case meant saying the first batty thing that came into my head, and hang the consequences. That's why I'd been giving Monsieur Cardin the same sort of treatment, and though I say it myself, he'd responded very well to Doctor Edmunson and her clever techniques. Anyway, I liked him. He was nice.

Back to the farmer, though. He was really making himself at home in the Cardin kitchen. Madame was pouring him coffee and pushing everything on the table in his direction: butter, jam, marmalade, baguettes. You name it, he had it thrust at him, and he certainly didn't have any hesitation in tucking in. Before you knew it there was hardly a morsel left on the table. He'd wolfed the lot.

It turned out that his name was Daniel, and that he worked at Tattlequack Farm. Madame proudly got out the eggs that I'd bought for her the other day, then between them Monsieur and Madame told Daniel the "Beau and the heroine" story. I sat back and waited for the congratulations to roll in, and you can imagine my dismay when instead of congratulations all I got was mirth. *Not again*, I thought. Can nobody take me seriously for more than two seconds?

"Daniel doesn't believe that it's possible to get past Beau without being at least bitten," Michelle explained slowly.

"But I did get past him."

Daniel didn't speak a word of English, so Michelle played interpreter for us.

"In France, when people see guard dogs in the yard they don't venture past them," was Daniel's first comment, which was obviously a dig at the English.

"In England, people don't either, but I've got a way with dogs, you see." I saw the amusement and the obvious disbelief in Daniel's eyes when Michelle translated for me, and it really bugged me. How dare he not believe me!

"What does he want? Proof?" I demanded impulsively. The moment the words were out of my mouth I regretted

183

them, but it was too late. Michelle was well into her translation.

"*Oui. Un demonstration!*" Daniel exclaimed. There was no need for Michelle to translate. We all knew what I'd let myself in for. I saw Jaimini close her eyes in horror, then open them and give me a withering look as if to say, "You really don't know when to keep your mouth shut, do you?"

There was just one possible get-out. Maybe Daniel wouldn't be available for the great demonstration until a date after we'd gone. I said a silent prayer, but Daniel was obviously very keen to get this thing organized.

"When?" Michelle translated for him. Before I could reply, though, Monsieur Cardin was saying something in a very serious tone. I asked Michelle to translate and she told me that her father thought that it was a very irresponsible thing to do, for me to prove that I'd been telling the truth. Apparently Monsieur Cardin was worried that I'd never do it a second time, and if the dog mauled me it would be terrible. I could have kissed him for saying that, but Daniel wouldn't let it go. He said he'd be there to make sure that I didn't come to any harm, but Monsieur Cardin was adamant that he wasn't going to allow me to do it, so that was the end of that. Or so I thought.

Later that morning Jaimini and I and Emma and Michelle went to the local cafe. I found that my heart was beating hard because I didn't want to see Thibault. The trouble was that now I knew how unpopular and horrible he was I couldn't possibly be friendly towards him and yet, strangely enough, a part of me was still really attracted to him, and I wasn't sure if I'd be able to resist talking to him, and that would make the others cross with me. So it would be easier all round if he simply wasn't there.

As soon as we walked into the place I had a quick look round and felt a big relief when I saw that he wasn't inside, but we'd only just got our drinks when he walked through the door looking cooler than ever. "Right, Luce, get a grip," I told myself. So I kept reminding myself of how rotten he'd been to Fen and Sophie, and how he'd been completely out of order to Nicholas for years. He saw me almost immediately and came straight over. I saw Jaimini's scowl, and Emma and Michelle were wearing similar expressions, so I felt as though I ought to at least try to look uninterested. But that was the problem: I *was* interested.

"*Bonjour, Lucy.*"

"Bonjour."

"Tu veux m'acheter un cafe?"

He was grinning all over his face. I wished I knew what he was on about. I looked at Michelle for help.

"He says do you want to buy him a coffee?" she translated for me in a withering voice, with a warning look in her eyes that said, "Don't even bother to answer him, Luce."

"Tell him I haven't got any money," I said.

"No, just ignore him," she replied. So as Thibault stood there waiting for a reply, the four of us studied our drinks as though it was part of an earth-shatteringly important experiment. When he realized he wasn't getting a reply and that, what's more, he obviously wasn't welcome at our table, he left us and went over to his friends, but occasionally he glanced in my direction then whispered something behind his hand to one of his mates. I hated the way he did that. It unnerved me.

We were on the point of going when he came strolling back over again with his three friends. They gave us all very cool, hard looks, then Thibault said something that sent shivers down my spine. I knew roughly what he'd said, because I recognized quite a few words, but I had to look to Michelle for an exact translation.

"He says he hears that you're a dog psychologist," Michelle told me with a big sigh, as though she could only just bring herself to bother to translate such a juvenile thing.

"What's that supposed to mean?" Jaimini asked, sounding very stroppy.

Michelle asked, and the reply came back as follows.

"He said that you've made a fool of yourself, spreading the story that you can get past the fiercest guard dog in Normandy without the dog moving a muscle."

"How did he find out about that?"

"I've no idea, and it doesn't really matter. Just ignore him, Luce."

"But I *can*, because I *did*. Tell him that, Michelle. Tell him I can."

I knew I was getting very shrill and childish, but it was getting on my nerves that no one believed me.

"Don't let him rile you," said Jaimini. "Just ignore him."

"You tell big lie," he said in slow English, with a scornful look on his face.

"It's not a lie," I replied, standing up and flashing my

eyes at him. Any remaining bit of attraction I'd ever felt for this boy had finally gone. I could have ripped his silly necklace off and dropped it into the dregs of Michelle's coffee, I was feeling so angry.

"Calm down, Luce," Jaimini warned me, but being me I didn't pay any attention to her wise words, of course.

"No, I'm not calming down. I'm getting accused of being a liar, and I'm not one," I snapped.

"*Fais-nous un demonstration*," he said, leaning forward with a challenging look in his eyes.

Not again. I was getting sick of this.

"No, Luce. Tell him to get lost," Michelle said. "You heard what my father said, and he's quite right. You'd be putting your life at risk. Don't be silly."

"*D'accord*," I said, meeting Thibault's challenging look defiantly.

"No, Luce. I'm not letting you," said Jaimini.

"*Non, Lucy*," said Michelle and Emma together, but I'd had enough. I'd managed to get past the dog once so I'd manage a second time, and then Thibault would have to eat his words.

I hadn't realized, but Thibault meant that he wanted the demonstration right there and then. He indicated to me that he wanted me to follow, and this sent Jaimini, Emma and Michelle into a blind panic. Michelle and Jaimini started talking urgently together. They were making quick plans because they could see that I was determined to go through with it. The plan was that Michelle and Emma would rush home and get their parents, while Jaimini was going to stay glued to my side and presumably carry on trying to persuade me not to go through with my foolish, headstrong plan. You see, I *knew* it was foolish and headstrong and yet still I had to do it. I was getting like Andy. Maybe I'd start to get a reputation as "the other daring one", instead of being called the crazy one. That would be good. That would give me some much-needed street cred.

Thibault was in a hurry. He wanted to get the demonstration over and done with before anyone turned up to prevent it from happening. One of his friends had a car, and the four of them along with Jaimini and I all squashed in. I sat in the back with Jaimini on one side and a boy on the other who was smoking so much I thought my lungs would explode. I also had to put up with Jaimini, who spent the whole of the three-minute journey telling me I was out of my tree and that I must *not* go and put myself in danger like this. She even threatened to go to a public phone box and phone up Mum and Terry. I just ignored that, because I knew she'd never do it. Anyway, she wouldn't have had enough money.

There was no stopping me now. I had to prove to Thibault and to anyone else who cared to watch that I did have some kind of power over dogs, and that I could get past Beau. There were only three things worrying me. One was that I wasn't sure whether the dog would be the same with an audience. It was important that he couldn't see anyone else. I had to be on my own. The other was that this was much later in the morning. What if the farmer and his wife suddenly appeared and accused me of trespassing on their land? At least that would put a stop to the demonstration. A part of me hoped that this would be the case, then I wouldn't be in danger yet I wouldn't lose face. The third thing that was worrying me – and I hardly dared to think about this – was that I didn't really have any special powers over dogs, I just liked to think I did. The whole idea that I've got a way with dogs comes from the time when a big hairy dog followed me home and wouldn't leave me alone. He's our dog now. We call him Harry.

It was as we were all getting out of the car that I began to have doubts but, of course, it was too late to say anything by then or I'd look a complete wally. I just prayed that the Blanchards would be in the yard and we'd all have to go away and forget the whole thing. Thibault's friend parked the car a little way away, presumably so the farmers wouldn't be alerted by the dog's barking and come out to see who it was. I was on the point of talking loudly when Thibault put a finger to his lips and, looking round at each of us individually, gave us our own personal warning not to make a sound. Only my hammering heart made any noise and I don't suppose anyone but me could hear that.

Thibault mimed that everyone was to stay back while he went to size up the situation. He silently and furtively walked up to the gate, then turned round and mimed that I was to approach the gate softly, but the others were not to move. When I was right by the gate, he moved back and joined the others, who were about three metres away, hidden from the dog's view by the end of the farmhouse. Beau was sitting in the centre of the yard exactly as he had been the last time. One look at the expression on Jaimini's face made me start praying silently but frantically.

Please let Monsieur and Madame Cardin come zooming up in their car, or otherwise please let the farmers appear and order us off their premises, I thought. But neither of these things happened and Thibault was flapping his hand at me as if to say, "Go on, get on with it." There was nothing for it. I had to face the music.

I opened the gate with trembling hands and the dog jerked his head. It was the tiniest of actions, but I figured that if he'd been able to talk, he would have been saying, "I don't believe this. I let you get away with it once, but this time you're for it!" I braced myself and felt a tiny shred of relief that at least Thibault and the others couldn't actually see the fear in my eyes because I had my back to them. The moment I'd had that thought, I realized that I mustn't show fear or Beau would pick it up and that would make him attack. I had to appear confident and in charge.

"Hello, Beau," I said in a soft, singsong voice. "It's me again. You remember me, don't you? Good old Lucy from England, who really thinks you're a great dog. I do, you know. I've told so many people about you."

I had taken three steps towards him during this ridiculous speech. Beau hadn't moved a muscle.

"What a handsome boy you are," I said as I took my next two steps. In two more steps I'd be level with him and after another two I'd be past him. Then what was I going to do? We hadn't actually stipulated the rules for the demonstration, but presumably as long as I got past him, then back out again, that would be enough. The trouble was, no one was watching. Thibault might refuse to believe that I'd done it. I took my eyes off Beau for a second to turn round and see whether I was being watched. I was.

Thibault and his three friends were peering round the side of the house. Only their heads showed, one above the other. Jaimini wasn't with them. I could imagine her cowering in a corner somewhere, praying that I'd come out of this escapade alive. As I turned back to Beau I felt sure I heard a car drawing up very smoothly and softly. I was right, because Beau reacted. He adjusted his two front paws and a low growl began from deep in his throat. The hair on my arms stood on end. Beau could sense that things were not right. He knew he was being watched, and though he was used to cars, they didn't usually arrive like this, soft and purring. Very slowly and very smoothly he began to stand up as I stood rooted to the ground, not knowing what to do, because it was clear now that I was in danger. Big danger.

Jaimini

I've been friends with Luce since we were both in year four at primary, and in all those years, no matter how ridiculous the situation that she got herself into, I could always see the funny side. Not this time, though. No way. My mind had been working frantically, trying to decide what on earth to do to stop this whole stupid thing from going ahead. Thibault made me sick and, in a way, I would have loved it if Luce could make him look an utter fool in front of his friends by proving him wrong. But not like this. To tell the truth, I hadn't been as concerned as

Michelle when the idea of the demonstration had come up in the cafe. I suppose it was because I'd never actually seen the dog, and also because I felt fairly sure that Luce wouldn't agree to do anything unless she was certain she could bring it off.

It was different now, though. I'd seen the Alsatian, and the sight of it sitting there ready to launch itself at any intruders made my knees tremble. I'd only taken a quick look, then I'd got back out of sight and just hoped that Michelle and Emma had managed to impress on their parents that they must come immediately, because Luce was in deep trouble.

It was such a relief when I saw the car appear round the corner. Whoever was driving was taking the precaution of going very slowly and quietly. As the car drew nearer I saw that it was Monsieur Cardin. Madame Cardin rolled down her window and asked me what was happening.

"Luce is in there with the dog," I said, in a shaky voice.

Monsieur Cardin went very pale and pulled over, then the four of them got out of the car, but didn't close their doors – they just pushed them to. At the same time, another car drew up behind theirs. Daniel clambered out. One of Thibault's friends turned round at that point and saw that they had company. He passed this piece of information on to the others and they all turned round to take a look, but only for a second. They were too intent on the action. I wondered what on earth was happening in the farmyard. I also wondered what on earth the Cardins or Daniel could do to help. Michelle whispered to me that they'd tried to phone the Blanchards the moment they'd heard what was happening, but there had been no reply.

Just when I thought I'd scream if this whole horrific episode didn't come to a close, I heard Thibault gasp, then his friends did the same. They straightened up and moved forward very slowly so that all four of them were in full view of the entrance to the farmyard. What *did* they think they were doing? This would surely make the Alsatian go mad.

"*Regardez!*" breathed Thibault, in a voice that sounded as though he was witnessing a miracle. Slowly, cautiously, the rest of us crept up to the gate to look.

Luce was kneeling down in the middle of the farmyard, stroking Beau, and Beau was lying down, docile and affectionate, his head on Luce's lap, his eyes staring up adoringly at her. For a moment she stopped her stroking action and Beau sat up abruptly. I took a sharp breath, but I needn't have worried. Beau's tail was wagging. He nuzzled his head into Luce's neck and her mass of hair hung over his eyes as she rested her head on his. I couldn't resist sneaking a quick look at Daniel. His jaw had dropped open. He was well and truly gobsmacked. And that's when Michelle took two photos, one of Luce and Beau, the other of Daniel. I couldn't wait to get them developed. We had the proof! Good old Luce.

Chapter 17

Tash

This is such a wonderful week. I suppose the trip to Disneyland has to be the highlight, but we've had loads of other wonderful times, too. I often wonder which moments will stick in my mind when I get back to England. I know one moment that will, and that's when Monsieur Leroi and Monsieur Leblanc shook hands with each other at the monkey reserve after two years of not speaking. I knew there would be loads of other memories for me to take home with me, too, and the others all felt the same.

Since Disneyland we'd had a day out with all the others in a vast and beautiful forest, where we'd been able to see deer and boars and all sorts of other wildlife. The six of us went round with an English guide, and I was really in my element, because I love everything to do with nature. I'm like Mum in that respect. There were beautiful log cabins dotted about all over the forest, and we met up with our French friends for an enormous picnic lunch in one of them. In the afternoon we went to a chateau, and in the evening we had a barbecue at Serge's and Marie-Jo's.

Everybody else offered their garden, but Serge and Marie-Jo insisted that they didn't mind, so we stayed there because it was easily the biggest and best place for us all to meet. Laurette's parents came to the barbecue. They were really nice.

The following day big preparations started for Celine's birthday party. The Leblancs had organized a catering firm to prepare and serve the food. The party was to take place in the village hall, which they called the *salle des fêtes*, the party room! For most of the day Celine and I, along with Katrine and Victoria, helped carry things over to the hall and decorate it. We also helped to set up a disco and what was needed for games.

Then in the afternoon Celine's parents insisted that Katrine and Victoria go to bed for a couple of hours, and she asked Celine and me if we wanted to do the same. I couldn't work out why on earth she thought we would want to sleep in the afternoon, but Celine explained that, in France, parties always go on till about five in the morning and that everyone joins in, from old great-grandparents to tiny little children! I was explaining how different it was in England, and how the adults nearly always had separate parties from the children, and she thought that was weird. The more I thought about it the more I liked the sound of the French system.

Celine and I decided not to bother to go to bed because we knew we wouldn't sleep even if we did. We were too excited. The thing Celine was really looking forward to was receiving lots of presents. Madame Leblanc had told me that I must on no account go spending my money on presents. Well, to be exact, she told Andy to tell me that on no account must I go spending my money. She also told the others there was absolutely no need to get Celine anything because she would be thoroughly spoilt by her relatives. In the end, though, the six of us clubbed together and bought a huge clip frame for Celine. We'd already taken tons of photos between us and we intended to take more at the party, so then we were going to get them developed in England and make copies of the best ones to send to Celine to complete her present. We'd already given her the frame, and she'd been really pleased with it, and thought the whole thing was a brilliant idea.

The thing that I was looking forward to the most was hearing Leah play her violin. Apparently at French parties, loads of people sing or tell jokes on a mike, and sometimes children show dances that they've learnt. Leah was really nervous and kept saying that it would be the wrong sort of place to be playing her violin, and that no one would appreciate it, and that everybody else would be better than her, and various other Leah-type anxieties. The rest of us tried to make her believe that she would be great, but she wasn't having any of it.

There was one thing that I was absolutely dreading about the evening. Celine only told me this piece of information at the last minute, because she'd been worried about my reaction – Aline had been invited! I was horrified when I found out.

"Aline! Why?" was all I managed to utter.

"Because two or three years ago she was my best friend. It's only in the past year that she's really changed and we've grown apart."

It took ages for Celine to tell me this in a mixture of French and English.

"Your *best* friend?"

"Yes. There was a group of us who always hung around together, and Aline was always in the group with Sophie and the others, so Maman invited her, because I hadn't really explained to her that things had changed. I don't talk to Maman as much as you talk to your mum, you see, so she didn't know what happened in England."

"But do you still like Aline?"

"No, not at all. She's got plenty of other friends. She doesn't need me. Her other friends don't know what she's really like, you see."

"But why didn't you tell your mum that you didn't want her at your party?"

"Because she'd already sent her an invitation ages ago. I did try to reason with her, though. I told her the whole story about how horrible she'd been to Leah in England, and also about what had happened at Disneyland. She pursed her lips and looked serious, but she didn't make any comment other than to say that she was sorry, it was too late now, and we'd all just have to make the best of it. She said Aline wouldn't think of misbehaving in a room full of adults at a party, because she wouldn't dare."

"Do you think your mum believed you about Disneyland?"

"I'm not sure. I know I shocked her, that's all."

There was nothing more I could say to Celine after that. I mean, it wasn't *my* party, but I knew it would ruin the evening for Leah. I couldn't decide whether to warn her or not. In the end I managed to tell Andy, and decided to leave it to her to tell Leah if she wanted to. Andy had just said "Hm" when I'd told her, and I knew she wouldn't say much more even if I pressed her, because that's how Andy is. My mum would say that she's one of those people who play their cards close to their chest. It means she doesn't give many of her thoughts away.

As the evening drew nearer, the problem of what to wear came up. Fen and Sophie, Jaimini, Luce and Emma all came round to Celine's place to get changed. Andy and Leah were meeting us at the village hall. Those two never seemed to worry too much about clothes anyway. Leah gave it a bit more thought than Andy did, but she always looks brilliant in whatever she wears, anyway. I could just imagine them out in the garden having fun with Jacques and Laurette until the very last minute, then rushing in and changing into clean jeans and lovely tops, then quickly brushing their hair and flying downstairs, saying, "We're ready!"

Fen was as bad as Andy and Leah (or as good, depending on how you looked at it), then I was probably next, then Jaimini, then Luce. Long after the rest of us were all ready, Luce was still taking things off and putting things on, fiddling about with her hair, adjusting her eyeshadow, and painting her nails. She'd chosen a beautiful vivid shade of blue nail varnish for Celine's party. She was wearing tight white hipster trousers and a bright blue top, and the biggest pair of earrings you've ever seen. She'd sprayed blue and green streaks into her hair out of a can. Emma had assured her it would wash out straight away, but Luce didn't care. She was just delighted that she'd managed to colour her hair so cheaply.

The rest of us were all wearing trousers or jeans. Mine were stripy grey and black hipsters, Jaimini wore stone-coloured jeans and a beautiful orange top, and Fen was wearing faded blue jeans and a blue and white stripy shirt. All the French lot were dressed quite similarly, so there wasn't a dress or a skirt in sight amongst all of us.

I was right about Leah and Andy. They didn't have a trace of make-up on, and told us they'd got ready at the last minute because they'd been late back from a day out. Leah had brought some make-up with her, and she went straight to the toilets and put it on. Her hair had been scraped back in a high ponytail, but when she came out of the loos it was hanging down her back. She looked beautiful. Lots of people stared at her, but Leah wasn't aware of it, you could tell. There are quite a few girls in our year at school, and in the year above, who really fancy themselves. You can see this look in their eyes, as though they think everyone's looking at them and thinking how wonderful they are. It makes me squirm to see girls acting like that, and I made a promise to myself that I'd never get like that.

When the party had been going on for about an hour and a half, I realized why it was that French parties went on so late. It was because they took so long to start. All Celine's relatives turned up, and the kissing and introductions, especially with the six of us there, took ages. Every time anyone came through the door, I was dreading it being Aline. She was coming with a friend, who also used to be a friend of Celine's, but she wasn't any more.

After a while I began to think happily that maybe they weren't coming after all. It would take a lot of guts to come to a party where you knew you were going to come across at least six people who hated the sight of you. On the other hand, I suppose Aline knew that Leah couldn't prove a thing. Aline could just deny the whole Disneyland episode, and also everything that had gone on in England. Anyway, there was no way that any of us could start saying nasty things about Aline at a party. It wouldn't be fair of us to risk ruining it. I felt more and more depressed. Aline was sure to turn up. I wondered whether Andy had told Leah, but I didn't get the chance to ask because Leah and Andy were together every time I looked.

Trestle tables were set up in the shape of a capital E, but, nobody sat down until the *aperitifs* were finished. *Aperitifs* are what Mum and her friends would call nibbles. There were masses of them, and we had to stop ourselves from tucking into them too much, because we were all beginning to feel full before the meal had even started. We'd been warned by various people that the meal would be huge, so we must go easy at the beginning to leave room for a bit of every course. But when we asked what the food was to be, all anyone said was "pork" as though the rest of the meal didn't really count.

Celine's mum had been right: she received some fabulous presents, including big things like her own television and a CD player. I felt quite relieved that we'd already given her our present. Nobody else gave small presents at all. That's another way in which the French are different from the English, at least in Celine's town. They don't seem to bother with ordinary children's parties. They just have parties for the important birthdays, which are ten, thirteen, eighteen, thirty, forty and so on in tens. But when they did have a party it was big and lavish and everybody clubbed together to buy the presents.

It was as we were all taking our places at the table that Aline appeared with her friend. They were both dressed up to the eyeballs and caked with make-up. And Aline wore her best sneer. I'm not usually so horrible when I describe people, but I couldn't help it this time, because I did *not* want Aline in the room at all. Immediately I looked at Leah for her reaction, but she'd not even noticed. Her fingers were drumming on the table and she had a familiar, distant look in her eyes. I recognized that look. She was going through her violin piece in her head. She was going to play on the same violin that Lisa had managed to borrow. It was propped up in a corner. Aline's eyes were taking in every single thing in the hall, and I saw her clock the violin. So did Andy. Our eyes met, then I heard Leah gasp.

"Oh, no! Look who's here!" she said, through clenched teeth.

"It's not a problem," said Andy. "We're all here. Just ignore her. Make out that you're completely unbothered by her presence. Act like the thing at Disneyland never happened. That'll confuse her."

"I can't."

"Try."

"OK, I'll try."

"We'll all do the same thing," I said.

"Good idea," said Andy.

Jaimini, Luce and Fen had tuned in to what we were saying, because all the children at the party had been put on the bottom stroke of the E together. Jacques was sitting next to Andy, and the spare seats were nearer to Leah than anyone else. Any second now Aline and her friend would be sitting in them, so we all did a quick swap so that it was Celine and Sophie who were sitting next to the spare seats.

Andy had explained to our penfriends that we were all going to be over-the-top nice and friendly to Aline, and they had all agreed that was a good plan. Nicholas was sitting next to Monsieur Leblanc, with a cousin of Celine's on his other side. The cousin was about the same age as Nicholas, so at least he'd got someone to talk to. He would have been bored if he'd had to sit with us thirteen-year-olds. Once when I looked his way our eyes met, and he gave me a lovely smile. I smiled back and tried not to blush.

"*Salut, Aline et Amelie,*" said Celine lightly. "*Ça va?*"

That meant, "Hi, how are you?"

Aline looked rather taken aback, then tried to recover, but I was pleased that she'd felt uncomfortable for a moment. Andy started chatting to her as though she was her long-lost best friend. The rest of us were terribly impressed. Luce is the terrific actor out of the six of us, but Andy deserved an Oscar for this performance of hers. The more Andy chatted away, the more Aline looked unsure of herself. I bet she was beginning to think that Leah must have kept the events of Disneyland to herself. Leah didn't say anything to Aline, but I saw her give her a shaky smile at one point, and I thought that must have taken a tremendous effort on her part. I'm not sure that I would have been able to do it.

I couldn't follow what Andy and Aline were talking

about most of the time, but then I suddenly heard the word "violin", or rather "*violon*", which was obviously the French way of pronouncing it. I guessed Andy was telling Aline that Leah was going to play later. Aline said *she* was supposed to be playing the keyboard. At least that's what I think she said.

The evening rolled on amazingly easily considering how much I'd been dreading it. By eleven o'clock we'd had three courses and the pudding looked as though it was arriving. There'd been no sign of any pork and I wondered whether I'd completely misunderstood. The music was playing softly behind us and I was beginning to relax. The sweet course was lemon sorbet, and some of the adults were having calvados tipped over it. Calvados is a very strong apple alcohol. When the waitress came to us we all said no to the calvados, except Aline, who told her friends in a loud voice that she always had calvados and she didn't know what the fuss was about because it wasn't all that strong when you were used to it. Andy translated all this for our benefit and we all pretended to be very impressed while secretly laughing at Aline for being so cocky.

Imagine our shock when five minutes after the sorbet dishes had been cleared away, the pork arrived. Andy explained that the sorbet course was called the "*trou normand*" and it was supposed to be a little interval to clean your palate so that you could carry on eating without feeling too full! I didn't think I wanted to eat much more, but I dutifully took a bit of pork and some lovely-looking onion sauce and a few chips. Leah was eating hardly anything. I guessed she was probably doubly nervous –

one because of Aline being there, and two because of the thought of standing up and playing her violin in front of all these people.

Finally, the meal ended and the music got louder. The main lights dimmed and the disco lights flashed around the room. Immediately loads of people got up from the table and started dancing. The French adults were excellent dancers, far better than any English people that I know. There was one particular young French couple rock'n'rolling absolutely fantastically. It looked just as good as the dancing from the film *Grease*. The young people mainly disco-danced like us, but out of all of them, French and English, Fen was the best. I was so proud of her. She's a fantastic dancer. Loads of people were watching her. Out of the corner of my eye I could see Aline trying to imitate her, but she just looked silly. I whispered to Leah, because she looked so worried and I wanted to take her mind off the violin.

"Look at Aline. Doesn't she look stupid?"

Leah looked, then nodded, and whispered back that if she'd known at Disneyland that she would be dancing in the same room with Aline only days later, she wouldn't have believed it. I glanced at Aline and she glared at me. It was a glare that was full of hostility, and it made my spine tingle. She'd realized that Leah and I were laughing at her. Immediately afterwards she went and sat down on her own.

"Uh-oh," I said to Andy. "Aline saw me whispering to Leah about what a useless dancer she is, and she's got that mad expression on her face again. Look, she's sitting down on her own."

Andy and I glanced over at the table, but then both of

us did a double take, because Aline wasn't sitting there. No one was sitting there. I looked round the whole hall, but it was so packed with people dancing and so difficult to see in the disco lighting that there was no way I could spot where Aline was.

"I'm going to find her," Andy said. "You stay with Leah."

Chapter 18

Andy

I had a gut feeling about where Aline was going. It made me feel angry just thinking about it. I decided that enough was enough, and that I wanted to pay that girl back in no uncertain terms. I was taking an enormous gamble, but I reckoned it was worth it.

"Madame Leblanc," I said softly. I tapped her on the shoulder to attract her attention, because she was deep in conversation with a couple of old ladies whom I'd been introduced to as great-aunts of Celine's.

"Andeee, *cherie*," she said, with a huge, welcoming smile. I guessed she'd probably had quite a few glasses of wine. I wasn't sure if that was a good or a bad thing for what I was about to tell her. Tash had told me that Madame Leblanc knew all about Aline, but that she hadn't wanted to get into a discussion about it. Celine figured that she *did* believe her, though, and she was cross with Aline. I was relying on this being the case.

"I'm sorry to interrupt you, but I think Aline is up to mischief."

It was at times like these that I was glad to be bilingual.

It was important to say exactly the right thing to Celine's mother.

"Up to mischief?" she questioned, raising her eyebrows and giving me what Leah would call a very straight look.

"I think she's planning on doing something else to upset Leah, and I think it could be something to do with the violin that Leah's borrowed."

"We had better go and see," said Madame Leblanc, laying great emphasis on every single syllable and looking very tight-lipped. She excused herself from the two old ladies and got up. "Where is this violin? And where is Aline?"

"The violin's in the corner. I'm not sure where Aline is."

I *was* pretty sure, actually, but I didn't want to say. Together we pushed our way through the dancing mass of people until we came to the corner of the room. It was a dark corner, which the disco lights didn't quite reach. There was only one person in the corner, and that person was bending down, with her back to the crowd.

"Aline," said Madam Leblanc icily. "What are you doing?"

Aline jumped up and we both instantly saw the nail scissors in her hand. On the floor, the violin case lay open and when we looked closely we could see that all four strings of the violin had been cut. Our timing was perfect. Aline had nowhere to turn now. She had been trapped and she was really writhing.

"You are despicable," Madame Leblanc said through clenched teeth. The anger on her face was almost as frightening as the anger my dad sometimes shows.

At that very moment the disco lights went off and the main lights went on. Celine's dad, who was oblivious to what was going on in our little corner, began to address the happy guests over the microphone. Madame Leblanc, Aline and I all froze like statues as we listened to his cheerful words, which seemed to have no place in our angry corner.

"We are so pleased to see you all at our daughter's thirteenth birthday party, and it is with extra pleasure that we welcome Tash, Celine's English *correspondante*, and her five charming English friends. We are particularly lucky that one of these girls is a fantastic violinist, and she will be entertaining us shortly."

I cringed as Madame Leblanc called out loudly, "No, she won't."

Immediately the whole room turned to face us in our corner. There was a sudden silence, into which came the noise of a pair of scissors being dropped to the ground. Everybody then lowered their eyes to see what had fallen, and Madame Leblanc bent down very dramatically, picked up the scissors and held them above her head.

"Unfortunately the strings of the violin have been cut, haven't they, Aline?"

The silence was unbearable. For some people it really *was* unbearable. They began to whisper behind their hands, but their eyes never left Aline's face. For a micro-second I felt sorry for her. This was the biggest, most public put-down she could have suffered. My pity didn't last for long, though, because there suddenly flashed through my mind a picture of Leah's frightened face as she ran from the Pirates of the Caribbean.

"I've got a violin," called out a tall girl of about twenty-one. "The English girl is welcome to borrow it."

"Bravo!" someone yelled, and then the whole place relaxed once more into the party mood.

"Please enjoy yourselves, everyone," said Monsieur Leblanc over the mike, his voice not quite so confident as it had been moments before. Then the disco lights came on again around the room as the music struck up loudly.

"I am now going to ask my husband to drive you home, young lady, and he will explain to your mother exactly why."

Aline hung her head, then said she was going to get her friend. She didn't make a move to go and find her, though, and I realized she daren't. I was on the point of offering to get her friend myself when I thought, *No, why should I?*

"Go and get your friend then, Aline, and while you're over there, don't forget to apologize to *my* friend, will you?"

She didn't say anything, but I knew she would apologize to Leah because she knew I'd check up later, and I think she was finally scared.

Leah

The later it got, the more worried I became, because I wanted to look nice for Celine's party as I would be in the public eye. I know the others have got the idea that I don't worry about looking good, but the truth is, I do. Luckily, I'd already decided what to wear, which was my black jeans and purple top, but I really wanted to wash my hair and put some make-up on. At least my hair had been tied back all day so it wasn't as greasy as it would have been if it had been loose. And I took my make-up with me to the party.

The moment we arrived at the *salle des fêtes*, I went into the loos and put some make-up on and let my hair down. I felt better for doing that, but I was still feeling very nervous about playing the violin. Lisa had checked up with the friend who had lent her the violin, and she said it was fine for me to take it to the party. Laurette said the violin would be perfectly safe in the corner of the room furthest from the stage, so that's where I left it.

I tried to relax into a party mood like the others were doing, but it was impossible. I kept on imagining the awful moment when Monsieur Leblanc would stand on the stage and announce that Leah Bryan would now play her violin. Then I imagined everybody carrying on talking amongst themselves because my playing was too boring for a party. The more I thought about it, the worse my state became.

It was ages before we all sat down to eat because people kept on and on arriving, and the first course was the *aperitifs* for which you stand up. Personally I couldn't eat a thing, so it made no difference if I was standing or sitting. When we did eventually sit down, all the children were on the same table, except Nicholas, who obviously counted as an adult and sat with his cousin on one side and Monsieur Leroi on the other. There were two spare places next to me, and Jacques was next to Andy. I was about to ask who the empty seats were for when Sophie and Celine swapped places with Andy and me. Then the nightmarish bit of the evening began.

Aline turned up. I couldn't believe my eyes. Andy obviously knew about it because she immediately started telling me not to worry, and also telling me how I ought to play my cards. It turned out that Celine and Aline used to be great friends, but Madame Leblanc hadn't realized that the friendship had faded away since the trip to England. There was nothing I could do, much as I really wanted to hide under the floorboards until the party was over.

Andy had persuaded all of our group, French and English, to be really friendly towards Aline to confuse her. When I saw her, though, I didn't think I'd ever be able to do that because I hated the sight of her, she'd been so horrible to me in England and France. She was the world's worst bully.

It was obvious she felt uncomfortable with us all being nice to her. She was suspicious and didn't know how to react at all. After a bit she began to keep herself to herself, only really talking to her friend. They'd both got tons of make-up on and it made me wish I hadn't bothered to put any on at all. I didn't want to have a single thing in common with this girl.

As the evening wore on and people were enjoying themselves eating and dancing, I just grew more and more nervous, wishing that we could get the dreadful moment over with. Then, hopefully, I'd feel better.

"Look at Aline. Doesn't she look stupid?" Tash whispered to me, covering her mouth with her hand so that Aline wouldn't know what we were saying. I knew Tash was only trying to make me feel better and I was grateful to her. I whispered something back and realized that Aline was watching us. She knew we were talking about her because she tossed her head and glared at me coldly, then walked away as though she couldn't bear to be dancing on the same floor as me.

A minute or two later I suddenly realized that Andy was nowhere to be seen. I thought she must have gone to the loo. Then I saw Monsieur Leblanc going up on the stage. He was clutching a mike and I knew that he was about to introduce someone singing or dancing or, horror of horrors, playing the violin. In a way I wanted to get my bit over with first, but on the other hand I felt so nervous by then that I wasn't sure I'd be able to play a single note.

Monsieur Leblanc was welcoming everyone, and I heard the word "Tash" very early on in his speech, then not long after, he said "Leah Bryan" and "*violon*". I felt like dying. The disco lights had stopped and the music had been turned off, then from the back of the room came the steely voice of Madame Leblanc. Along with the rest of the room, I turned round to see that Andy was with Madame Leblanc, and so was Aline. A feeling of horror swept round the room at whatever Madame Leblanc had just said and, in the silence that followed, something dropped on to the floor. I couldn't make out what it was, but Madame Leblanc held up a pair of scissors and my face went white as I realized what had happened. This was history repeating itself. Aline had cut the strings of the violin just like someone once did to me out of spite in England. I thought I was going to faint, and Tash led me to the table, then one of the guests called out something about a violin and Celine was at my side, telling me that I could borrow another one.

The swirling lights and the music came back on and I began to wonder whether I had dreamt the whole awful incident. Andy returned and told me that Monsieur Leblanc was taking Aline and her friend home, and that she could guarantee that Aline would never bother me again. I didn't ask Andy how she knew that, but I believed her.

It was twenty minutes later that I had to play the violin. I stood on the stage quaking and trembling and wondering why everybody was so silent when I'd expected them to be chatting, completely uninterested in a foreign girl with a violin. Luce had once told me that when she got nervous on the stage she just took a quick glance round the audience and imagined that they'd all got no clothes on, which always made her want to giggle and forget her nerves. I tried this trick, but all I could see was a sea of smiling faces. The last face I saw before raising my bow was Victoria's. She was in a world of her own, pretending she was on the stage, because she was looking very serious, and her arms were in position as though holding the violin in one hand and the bow in the other. As I raised my bow, she raised hers, and that made me smile. Then I played.

I don't really remember how I played or how I felt, because I was concentrating on the sound of the violin. When you're playing on a violin that you're not used to, you have to work hard at it to make every note come out how you want it to. It was a lovely violin, with a much nicer tone than the one that Lisa had lent me. When I'd finished the piece I let my bow hang down at my side and saw that Victoria had done the same thing. I wondered if she'd been imitating me all the way through, and that made me smile again. I can honestly say that at that moment I felt happy. It was all over. The audience were still clapping, even though I felt as though I'd been finished for ages. They were still smiling, too. But all I wanted to do was eat. I was starving!

Fen

I loved Celine's party. Dancing is practically my favourite thing, and I knew I'd got hours and hours to dance away. I wished I'd not eaten quite so much, though.

There was only one thing spoiling this wonderful party, and that was the presence of the hateful Aline. I didn't know how she dared to show her face after what she'd done at Disneyland. I know it's a dreadful thing to say, but I positively enjoyed seeing her humiliated in public. She deserved everything she got. I felt sure it was Andy who had set it up. Good old Andy – she's full of cunning plans.

When Leah began to play I forgot all about Aline. It's impossible to think about anything else when Leah's playing. It's almost as though the sound she's making is acting like a magnet to your ears, and you just have to keep listening. Time and time again I've seen the shock on people's faces when she first starts playing. They must have an idea in their heads of how it's going to sound, and then when she begins to play, they're amazed because the sound is too good for a thirteen-year-old to make. I couldn't resist sneaking a subtle look round the audience. It was as I thought. They were all mesmerized. Leah has no idea of the power she's got. No idea.

When she'd finished, the place erupted. She just stood there and smiled while everybody clapped. I was so proud of her. I noticed that Laurette had got tears in her eyes, then I glanced over at Victoria and saw that she was bowing in a very dignified manner as though *she* had just been entertaining everyone with her wonderful music. I couldn't help laughing.

Jaimini

The party got better and better, and as I clapped and clapped for Leah, I thought it couldn't possibly improve any more. I think the moment that will always stick in my mind, though, was when Luce danced a waltz with Monsieur Cardin. I had never realized that it was common knowledge about his mental breakdown. Maybe people didn't know exactly what had happened to him, but they certainly realized that something had been wrong, because the entire hall came to a standstill to watch the amazing sight of a crazy English girl dancing with Monsieur Cardin, who was normally so quiet and sad and strange. I watched as the expressions on everybody's faces changed from gobsmacked and horrified to puzzled, then from slightly unsure of what was happening to that sort of penny-dropping look, then to real joy!

Everyone stood back so that Luce and Monsieur Cardin

had the dance floor to themselves. They were talking and laughing as they danced, and then everyone clapped like mad. Things gradually went back to normal after that, and the dance floor filled up again.

It came as quite a shock when Monsieur Leblanc went back up on to the stage and asked the English girls to "approach the micro", as he put it. Leah stayed on the stage and the rest of us exchanged looks of alarm, then we got up reluctantly and did as we were told. He wanted us to say a few words each, because all the French guests found us so "*charmantes*". In any other situation this would have been really embarrassing, but somehow, in this crazy party atmosphere, we didn't really mind, especially when all the guests cheered and wolf-whistled at Monsieur Leblanc's suggestion. The others all seemed to think that I should go first, but I thought it should be Leah. Leah said she didn't want to speak at all, because she'd done her bit by playing, so in the end I agreed to say something. I wasn't sure if I was supposed to be stuttering something in French or speaking in fluent English.

"*En français, hein?*" said Monsieur Leblanc with a wink, and the answering cry came from the guests, "*En français! Oui!*" but I knew I wouldn't be able to say what I wanted to say in French so I asked Andy to translate as I spoke. This meant that I only said a bit at a time over the mike, then I handed it to Andy, and she translated, and so on.

"I've loved my stay in France. I've been very lucky to have been with the Cardins. I've made a lovely new friend in Michelle Cardin, Emma's sister, and I know we'll keep in touch. I'll take loads of wonderful memories back to England with me, but I think the moment that will stick in my mind more than any other is the sight of my best friend, Luce, kneeling down and stroking the Blanchards' Alsatian in the middle of their yard, when they were nowhere in sight."

As Andy translated this, a gasp went round the audience and I could hear their exclamations of disbelief, but Madame Cardin chipped in at that point and told everyone that she had seen it too, and she hadn't believed her eyes. "*Ces jeunes anglaises-la sont tres douees*," she added, which Andy quietly translated for us as, "These English girls are very gifted."

Luce

I couldn't wait for my turn on the mike. I'd had one-and-a-half big glasses of wine and I felt like singing songs, telling jokes and generally entertaining the guests.

"I've had the most fantastic time in France," I began, and I was about to continue when Jaimini grabbed the mike from me and handed it to Andy. I'd completely forgotten that hardly anybody could understand me, so I waited for Andy to translate, then continued: "Disneyland was fantastic, all French boys are lovely [a big whistle went up when Andy translated that bit!], all French girls are lovely [a big cheer followed that comment!], all French ladies are lovely [a round of applause!] and all French – " I handed the mike to Andy to translate those three words, because I knew they all thought I was going to say "men are lovely," but when Andy handed it back, I continued "dogs are lovely," which got a big laugh. Then finally I said, "And I don't know about all French men, but I do know who my favourite French man is." Andy translated that bit and the guests started calling out names of attractive film stars and singers. I waited till they had stopped, then I said, "Monsieur Cardin." The biggest cheer of all went up when I said that. And I added, "I hope he's saving the last dance for me."

I knew I was being outrageous but I didn't care. Andy translated my words and they received a laugh, as I'd guessed they would.

"Of course," Monsieur Cardin called back to me as he blew me a kiss. That went down even better on the clapometer, and as I looked round, I could tell that everybody knew I'd really meant what I'd said – and I did. I really did. A lump came into my throat. I was going to miss him.

Fen

"I got off to a terrible start with Monsieur and Madame Leroi, but now we're the best of friends!" I began, when Andy handed the mike to me.

I don't know if word had got round about Sophie and me being drunk, but all the laughing guests seemed to find my opening remark hysterically funny.

"The other people who are now the best of friends are Celine's parents and Sophie's parents."

A definite gasp of amazement went round when I said that, so obviously this was the first anyone else knew about the big make-up.

218

"Sophie, Celine, Tash and I would like to congratulate ourselves just a little bit for helping with that!" That raised another laugh. "And I want to thank everybody who's made my stay in France so much fun, especially Sophie's family."

Tash

There was only me left, and I felt very self-conscious. The others had managed to speak so easily, and I was sure I'd mess up my bit.

"I just want to thank Monsieur and Madame Leblanc for being so welcoming and kind to me. I'll never forget my stay in France, and I really hope that all our French friends will come and visit us in England again, and that we'll all come back to France, too. I can't say what my best moment was, because it's all been so wonderful, and – "

I couldn't carry on. I felt close to tears. I was thinking ahead, and knowing how much I'd miss everyone, especially Nicholas, and yet Nicholas and I had been no greater friends to each other than any other two people. He probably just looked at me as one of the six English girls – nothing special. Andy had translated up to "so wonderful, and. . ." so I *had* to carry on because everybody was waiting.

Then before I knew it, there was Nicholas on the stage beside me, with his arm round me and the mike in his hand. He spoke in French, but Andy whispered into my ear what he was saying.

"This is the kindest, loveliest girl in the world, and just

as Lucy will have the last dance with Monsieur Cardin, I hope that Tash will have the last dance with me."

He then handed the mike to Andy, turned his back to the audience so that he was blocking me from their view, and put his arms round me. You know I said I couldn't say which was my best moment? Well, I can now!

Andy

Everybody had spoken. I handed the mike to Monsieur Leblanc, and he addressed the guests.

"And finally, the only one who hasn't spoken for herself, Mademoiselle Agnes Sorrell," he announced grandly. I'd thought I was going to be let off, but apparently not. I wasn't at all prepared, and anyway, I don't like speeches, and how could I possibly say what was in my mind? That I'd also had a wonderful time, and that when I went back to England I'd miss Jacques more than I think I've ever missed anyone in my life? I knew it wasn't very original any more, but all I wanted to do was dance with Jacques for the rest of the evening. I smiled down at him from the stage and he gave me that special smile back. I've never seen him give that smile to anyone else. It was just for me. I lifted my shoulders and raised my palms as if to say, "I don't know what to say."

Jacques nodded at me slowly and I took that to mean that he understood how I felt. That was the best thing about my relationship with Jacques. We understood each other completely. And Marie-Jo knew how we felt about each other, too. She'd even helped us to find ways of seeing each other more often. In fact, she'd already booked a holiday in England for the whole family in three weeks' time, and she'd also pointed out that it would be very good for me to come over with my dad on the odd business trip. "You can always stay with us, Andy," she had said, with a twinkle in her eye.

But here I was with the mike in my hand and nothing to say.

"We'll be going soon, but we'll be back again before you know it!" I finally said. "So, *merci tout le monde. A bientot, la France*. See you soon."

"*A bientot*," rang out the voices of all my friends as we stood round the mike in a tight little group.

"*A bientot!*"

Also in the Cafe Club series by Ann Bryant

Have you read?
Go for It, Fen!
Leah Discovers Boys
Luce and the Weird Kid
Jaimini and the Web of Lies
Andy the Prisoner
Tash's Secrets
Fen's Revenge
Leah in Trouble
Luce's Big Mistake
Jaimini and the Mystery of Evi Bligh
Andy in the Dark
Tash and the Fortune-Teller
Fen Gets Jealous
Leah's Nightmare

Look out for:
Luce Finds Her Hero
The Cafe Club Special:
Secrets and Dreams